The disguise was perfect.
Absolutely nothing could go wrong.

FLAWED DOGS

THE SHOCKING RAID ON WESTMINSTER

FLAWED DOGS

THE NOVEL

WRITTEN AND ILLUSTRATED BY
BERKELEY BREATHED

PHILOMEL BOOKS
PENGUIN YOUNG READERS GROUP

Thanks to my pal Jean-Leon Gerome for letting me improve
on his "Pollice Verso" of 1872.—B.B.
The illustrations on pages iii and facing page 184 are re-envisioned from the author's picture book:
Flawed Dogs: The Year-End Leftovers at the Piddleton Last Chance Dog Pound
(Little, Brown), © 2003 Berkeley Breathed.

PHILOMEL BOOKS
A division of Penguin Young Readers Group.
Published by The Penguin Group.
Penguin Group (USA) Inc., 375 Hudson Street, New York, NY 10014, U.S.A.
Penguin Group (Canada), 90 Eglinton Avenue East, Suite 700, Toronto, Ontario M4P
2Y3, Canada (a division of Pearson Penguin Canada Inc.).
Penguin Books Ltd, 80 Strand, London WC2R 0RL, England.
Penguin Ireland, 25 St. Stephen's Green, Dublin 2, Ireland
(a division of Penguin Books Ltd).
Penguin Group (Australia), 250 Camberwell Road, Camberwell, Victoria 3124, Australia
(a division of Pearson Australia Group Pty Ltd).
Penguin Books India Pvt Ltd, 11 Community Centre, Panchsheel Park,
New Delhi—110 017, India.
Penguin Group (NZ), 67 Apollo Drive, Rosedale, North Shore 0632, New Zealand
(a division of Pearson New Zealand Ltd).
Penguin Books (South Africa) (Pty) Ltd, 24 Sturdee Avenue, Rosebank,
Johannesburg 2196, South Africa.
Penguin Books Ltd, Registered Offices: 80 Strand, London WC2R 0RL, England.

Published simultaneously in Canada. Printed in the United States of America.
Design by Katrina Damkoehler. Text set in ITC Galliard.

Library of Congress Cataloging-in-Publication Data
Breathed, Berkeley.
Flawed dogs : the shocking raid on Westminster /
Berkeley Breathed. p. cm.
Summary: After being framed by a jealous poodle,
a dachshund is left for dead, but comes back with a group of mutts from
the National Last Ditch Dog Depository to disrupt the prestigious
Westminster Kennel Club dog show and exact revenge on Cassius the poodle.
[1. Dogs—Fiction. 2. Dog shows—Fiction.] I. Title.   PZ7.B7393Fl 2009
[Fic]—dc22   2009002638

ISBN 978-0-399-25218-1
1 3 5 7 9 10 8 6 4 2

All animals dream.
But only dogs dream of us.

AUTHOR'S NOTE

The recently released *Congressional Report* on the Westminster Dog Show Riot is rubbish.

The source of that day's injuries and property destruction is not so easily written off to the violent reaction to "a panicked poodle peeing in the punch," as President Obama famously said when trying to calm the anxious nation.

This country has prided itself in facing its most traumatic events with the courage that comes from the unblinking truth, no matter how shocking.

After months of careful, courageous research into the lives of those responsible for this disaster, I am happy to deliver the true story to you now.

BERKELEY BREATHED

ONE

– SCENT –

The Rough-Handed Man carried him through crowded rooms empty of heat and kindness. The hands were shaking, but not from the cold. He became aware that the man was whispering to him: "It's our turn, little buddy, little tough guy. I know you can do it. I need you to do it. You're not so big, but you got a big stubborn heart bigger'n all of . . . of . . ."

The voice paused.

"Well, it's bigger'n mine."

He was small for a dachshund and was being held upright like a fat salami on end. His bony spine lay against the man's chest, his front feet bobbing before him. His broken rib required that he be carried this way. His fourth leg was not a leg at all but a steel soup ladle taped to his stump.

He curled his tongue up to lick his nose, dry and cracked from the cold. He was aware of being carried past more men—all mutts and mongrels, no purebreds—bustling and shoving about him with arms tattooed, grimy, wet.

Human-being smells enveloped him like a foul blanket: Smoke. Sweat. Chewing tobacco. Alcohol. Roasting meat.

And money.

The human beings' money smells of all those other things. *Among all the stuff they love so—cars, kids, wood floors, driveways, socks, hair, teeth, feet, plums—only their money they don't wash,* he thought.

They should.

And this time, it smelled of something else.

Something new.

He couldn't identify it, this scent so unfamiliar. Long ago in a different life he could put a nose to the June breeze and tell you that the marigolds in the North Meadow had bloomed and new paint was on a fence some-

where and the furry-shoed Fat-Fingered Lady three miles down the road had just pulled a blackberry pie from the oven, sprinkled it with nutmeg and then farted.

But here, now, he didn't know this new scent. He knew he didn't like it. He also didn't care. He was past caring about anything.

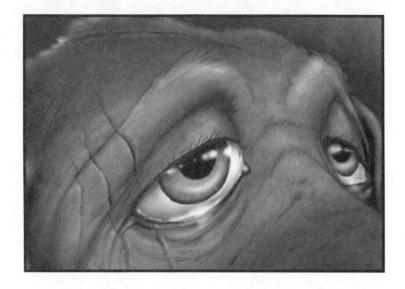

The man bore him through the jostling crowd, down some stairs, into more darkness, before entering a large space with a soaring ceiling filled with more men in shadow that he could not see but he could smell. And hear.

They shouted and argued and spoke harshly and waved paper in their hands. There it is again. Money.

He was lowered over a plywood wall formed in a circle, down farther until he felt dirt below his three paws. Dirt. At the bottom of a room in a building at the edge of a concrete city, how strange to feel dirt.

He would have thought about this more if he hadn't raised his eyes to see fifty pounds of bull terrier opposite him, five body lengths away, both front feet lifted off the ground. A reddening human hand held the collar and much of the huge beast's weight as it strained forward, the muscles of his neck bulging and looking to explode. Pulses of hot mist shot into the frigid air from a gaping pink throat: a slobbering murderous locomotive building up steam. The eyes were unblinking and wild and fixed forward on a single point opposite the terrible mouth.

"You want to kill me," the dachshund said aloud.

"I do," said the other dog.

"Isn't there anything you'd rather do instead?"

The big bull terrier stared at him, thinking hard. He'd never considered that question.

But the dachshund understood now why he was here, in this dirt, in this pit.

He looked up and found the face of the Rough-Handed Man staring down at him, looking crazy scared. "Ya gotta fight, little buddy!"

Fight.

The man might have just as well said, "Float." Or, "Fry up a haddock." Better would be, "Faint."

He backed up until the wood planks found his tail, which folded below his rump as he pushed back, back.

At that moment he also knew what that new smell was. He looked down and saw it, a dark crimson ribbon woven amidst the filthy dirt and food wrappers.

It was blood. It was life.

But here, spilled and dried in this terrible place, it was death.

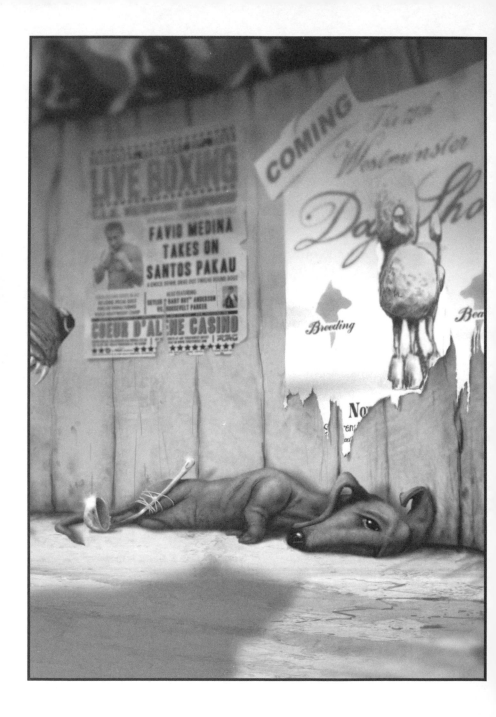

And here, finally, he knew it was the end of a long, unexpected road. He would go no further. *Here I stop.*

And here I die.

Slowly, he dropped his head and laid his long bony back down along the curved wall, three stubby brown legs out straight as if stretched on a porch on a hot day.

One of the men in the mob yelled out: "He's a-gonna take a snooze!"

The crowd hushed into stunned silence as they stared.

Then they exploded into twice the frenzy, waving their smelly money harder. The raging dog across the pit twisted against his restraints. The Rough-Handed Man leaned over the wall, waving at him: "Up! Get up! UP! YA CAN'T LIE DOWN, LITTLE BUDDY!"

Watch me.

He dropped the side of his head flat against the dirt and looked sideways at the end of his world. He looked for something—anything—to fix his eyes on rather than the drooling, corrupted fighting machine soon to be upon him with its broken fury. His gaze went up to a single arc bulb overhead flooding the pit with light. Blue, cold and blinding; yes, this would do.

He stared at it and then closed his eyes. A new light took its place: the sun on a cobalt sky above the rolling green hills of another time and another world long ago. It was dazzling. *It's warm,* he thought, and closed his eyes tighter. He traveled back and felt wild grass below his paws and breathed other, less cruel scents on the wind while he ran in a blur through a forest of exploding dandelions. And he heard her voice calling his name. "Sam! Sam the Lion!"

Her voice!

Heidy.

Above in the roiling crowd, the Rough-Handed Man looked down in the fighting pit at the three-legged dachshund lying still on its side, eyes clenched shut, and saw something out of place. He squinted and leaned closer and looked.

No. Can't be. Not here and not on a dog:

A smile.

TWO

- UP -

Three years before . . .
In another time and another place . . .
Late August.

Heidy McCloud sat in the last row of the airplane as it taxied toward the small terminal and looked out the left-hand side window, changing her life forever.

Years later she suggested to other people whose lives

were on a crummy, hopeless dead-end path that a good thing to do is to look in the direction exactly opposite of which you were *going* to look. Catch life by surprise.

If she'd been seated on the right side of the plane, she would have seen only fat green hills dotted with fat cows. She would have wondered if cows attacked. She would have seen the elegant sign over the terminal door greeting visitors:

Piddleton, Vermont—Home of The World's Most Beautiful Dogs.

"Oh, brother. I don't belong *here*," she would have said with a grimace of remembrance. A single word would have occurred to her:

RUN!

And she would have dropped her bags the moment she'd left the plane and made a dash in the direction of Fiji, where she'd read somewhere that fourteen-year-olds were considered fully grown and could legally lie around the beach their entire lives eating Fruit Roll-Ups.

But Heidy didn't look out the right side window because back in St. Paul, Minnesota, the nuns of the St. Egregious Home for Troubly Girls had strapped her in row 40—on the left. They had assumed correctly that it was the farthest point from the cabin door on the right and she'd have trouble getting to it when it occurred to her

somewhere over Indiana that a pleated school skirt might make a decent parachute.

So it was the left window that she pressed her face on and looked down.

A dozen dog crates were stacked on the tarmac. Each had a shipping label. *Like boxes of tomatoes,* thought Heidy.

They had just been off-loaded from the cargo compartment of a large plane, waiting to be picked up by their new Piddleton owners. Each held a different kind of dog—the world's most beautiful dogs—all of whom were sleeping or looking stupidly at the air molecules go by.

Except one.

The dachshund looked up through the chrome bars at the young human female. *"Ah. They've got you too,"* he said aloud. The girl's face pressed against the glass of the airplane above him. He sighed and added: *"Your crate is better."*

The dachshund knew almost nothing about people. He knew the rubber boots of the one that used to clean his kennel and bring him his kibble, but he'd never spoken to the man. The last three hours in the plane only added to his life experience a plastic shipping crate, the smell of jet exhaust and the sounds of turbine engines.

And now a new young human face was looking down at him. He stared back. As he stared at her and she stared at him, fifty feet and millions of years of evolution separated them. The sight of the human girl inspired the first murmurings of a primordial dog instinct rumbling deep inside his dog skull, and a single thought slowly rose to pop into his dog brain:

"I want," he said, *"one of those."*

Suddenly a much different face filled the cage's opening, peering through the bars one inch away from his nose. It was much older and rounder and smelled of perfume, hair spray and broccoli and bacon quiche. It squealed, "My handsome boy! My HANDSOME boy!"

A large squarish woman in a hairy blue chinchilla fur coat and hat unlatched the cage door and pulled the young dachshund out, holding him up high for a first inspection. She rolled up her coat sleeves and stretched his torso, arching his back, while one hand clasped his muzzle, holding him high. She examined backbone, neck, shoulders, forehead, rump, teeth, eyes—did they align perfectly? She cocked her head, closed one purple eyelid and sighted down his nose. "Goooooorgeous! Just what I ordered! Straight and true!" she purred. She squeezed the dog's thighs.

Heidy watched from inside the plane above. She'd seen holiday shoppers inspect something else in the very same manner. What was it . . . ?

A Christmas ham.

On an instinctual level, the same thought occurred to the dachshund:

"NO, NO! Don't eat me, furry human!" he cried out, but the vice-like fingers held his mouth shut. A whimper emerged. His eyes could move, though, and he could see that the large woman must have fallen down stairs recently.

Her lips, nails, nose, cheeks and eyes were discolored into horrifying shades of purple. He shuddered at what monstrous hues might glisten on her other, unseen parts.

Suddenly the woman froze, her eyes locked to the top of his head.

"Good Lord 'n' holy butter! The cranial Duüglitz

tuft!" she said. A shaking finger reached out and touched a wisp of fur curling up from a point at the top of the dachshund's skull. Pierre Duüglitz was an eighteenth-century Austrian breeder who died without fulfilling his life's dream of producing a lime-green-colored dachshund. Instead he left behind a highly prized genetic abnormality that forever carries both his name and his eternal shame:

A little curly wisp of hair atop the head.

For the large woman in the chinchilla coat, it was the holy grail of dachshundom. She spun around and faced an airport man in white overalls behind her. She thrust the dog into the man's face. "Look! The Duüglitz tuft! THE DUÜGLITZ TUFT!!"

My name is Duüglitz, thought the dog.

"Oooooohhhh . . ." whispered the great woman in an ecstatic gargle growl of awe. "This one will *finally* win me the *Westminster championship!*"

The man rolled his eyes. "Mrs. Nutbush, as usual you'll have to wait until his shipping papers are processed. You can pick him up in cargo in a few minutes."

"Ah, well, there it is," Mrs. Nutbush said, and with a flourish placed the dog back into his crate. She bent down and put her face to the bars. "Mommy's little world champion!" She smiled broadly, but the dachshund noticed that she wasn't looking at his eyes, but rather at his tuft. "BeeYOOtiful," she purred. "I'll be back for you, sweet pea!"

She loped off. Bounced, really.

The dog stood in the crate, dazed, her words of doom still ringing in his ears: *"I'll be back!"*

He looked the other way and saw a green ocean of grass in the distance. It rippled like inviting waves. Waves a dog could run through forever.

Then he looked down to the latch on the crate's bars.

In a crisis, dogs can be simple in their thoughts. In this case he had just one:

OUT!

He tried to unhook the latch with his teeth. They weren't reaching. Tongue. Use the tongue! He wrapped it around the strange loop of metal and yanked sideways. Hard! Harder! He muttered: *"Slippery . . . stupid . . . c'mon, ol' Duüglitz Tuft, get a grip on it . . . out out out . . . OUT!"*

As he struggled in panic, his eyes happened to go back up to the window of the plane opposite, where the young human female's face still peered down at him. He couldn't hear, of course, but she was mouthing something behind the glass:

"Up," she was saying. "Pull it *up*."

THREE

— GROSS —

A few minutes later Heidy's bags banged about her knees as she walked down the plane's stairs. Before entering the terminal, she looked back at the dachshund, still in the dog crate twenty feet away. She stopped, checked to see if anyone was watching and stepped away from the yellow dotted line on the tarmac meant to keep people from doing exactly what she was doing.

She approached the stack of animal shipping boxes and

scanned their panting contents. There were every variety and shape and exotic breed. It was like a sidewalk fruit stall of dogs.

She found the dachshund, bent down and looked into the cage. He stopped biting the latch and looked up into her eyes, surprised that the young human being had gotten out of her own crate so easily. Heidy leaned her face in close to the bars.

"Hello, weiner dog."

He was nervous. But he was polite:

"Hello, hairless lips."

She pointed to the latch. "You're doing it wrong."

The dog suddenly forgot about escape and his questions poured out: *"What breed are you? You smell good! How do you keep rain out of those ears? How can you sniff the ground with that little nose? Your eyes are greenish. Do you see everything greenish? Do you have fingers on your other two feet? Do you eat kibble?"*

Heidy furrowed her brow. "I'm sorry. I don't understand dog."

"Here. Try this," he said.

The dachshund then did something that would change the rest of *his* life:

He kissed her.

More precisely, he licked her under the nose.

Not on the mouth, with the common paint-roller application of dog spit. The Big Kahuna, as Labradors call it. No, this was a gently executed upward swipe of the last quarter inch of tongue on the tiny band of flesh between the nostrils: the forbidden promised land of dog affection.

It is a gesture weirdly, wholly unique among an entire planet of animal types. A person may place his or her face before that of a panda bear, parrot, warthog, whale, lizard, elephant, trout, lemur, llama, monkey, rhinoceros, bunny, ferret, hamster, horse, house cat or domesticated dik-dik, but none of those will do what a dog will:

Kiss.

Unless the person's face is covered with jam. Or in the case of the cat, mouse intestines. Neither counts.

No, only a dog will smooch a human being. And he'll aim the kiss for the lips but be happy with a nose, chin, ear, neck, toe or buttock. Unlike grandmothers, dogs are not fussy.

In Heidy's case, it was under the nose.

She stood up straight, as if slapped. The dachshund looked equally shocked.

Neither knew it at the time, but a line had been crossed that could not be uncrossed—a running leap over the chasm of ignorance and misunderstanding between species and worlds . . . and a baby step taken into life's endless possibilities for wonder and joy and surprise that could no more be reversed than one's first taste of chocolate.

A dog kiss.

"That was completely gross," said Heidy.

With a flourish she wiped off the little amount of moisture with a sleeve—really, it was nothing—above her upper lip without looking away from the dachshund, who continued to stare at her. She spun around and walked briskly toward the terminal door.

But not before flipping the crate's latch upward and off.

FOUR

– MOO –

"I'm Mrs. Beaglehole," said an enormous elegant woman, whom Heidy mistook for a trained red cow. She stood stiffly just inside the airline terminal doorway, hands clasped, figured Heidy, about where her udder should be.

Mrs. Beaglehole blinked rapidly and looked down at the girl. "Miss Heidy McCloud, I presume. I now run your uncle's dog ranch. Welcome to Piddleton." She held out a

long hand. Heidy reached for it carefully with her own while eyeing the woman's toothy mouth. Cows attack.

"And welcome to your new life," Mrs. Beaglehole said, folding her hands again. "Your uncle is so very interested in seeing you again. Maybe with your hair brushed. How old were you again when you last visited him here? Thirteen?"

"Six," said Heidy. The woman snorted and pretended not to hear.

"He has great plans for you, you know."

"I don't like dogs," said Heidy. She thought she should put that out there early. Mrs. Beaglehole looked as if she'd been stuck with a knitting needle.

"Not like dogs! Why?"

Heidy looked back at the woman with equal shock. Did this ridiculous human heifer really not know that it was because of dogs . . . *DOGS!* . . . that her parents had died when she was a little kid? That it was because of DOGS that her criminally negligent uncle had dispatched her to stew with the mutant nuns at St. Egregious for all these torturous years? She didn't know that it was because of DOGS that Heidy's life was now shredded like one of her stupid uncle's giant canvas chewtoys?

Apparently not, concluded Heidy.

"I don't like dogs," she finally said. "Because they always need a bath."

Mrs. Beaglehole's smile tightened with annoyance and spread so wide that Heidy worried the ends of her mouth might stretch all the way around her neck and meet, allowing the mighty head to spring off and hit the ceiling.

"Dogs don't need baths *here,*" said Mrs. Beaglehole. "Unlike children. How you must be so looking forward to *yours.*"

Heidy stopped listening because she'd noticed something peculiar about Mrs. Beaglehole as she talked: with her head cocked ever so slightly to the left, the woman had one eye closed and the other focused on the center of the girl's face. She was sighting Heidy's nose for straightness. Exactly like the blue-furred woman had looked at the dachshund.

Heidy sighed and rolled her eyes. She looked past Mrs. Beaglehole and through the huge terminal windows, looking hard for the mountains of Fiji.

But she didn't see Fiji outside. She saw the dachshund out of his crate, crouched at the base of a pile of luggage on the tarmac outside, waiting to lunge for freedom.

A lion in the bush! thought Heidy, smiling.

Her first smile that day.

She watched the dog make a dash for the tarmac fence, but several workers cut him off, sending him into another group having lunch. His forward momentum took him straight up the leg of the first man, past his chest and up his face, which had several french fries sticking out of it. Dogs are creatures of survival, so he instinctively grabbed them all with his teeth as he climbed. Hooking a rear paw into the man's open mouth, he pushed himself onto the top of the man's head. The man flailed, as if being attacked by a fruit bat.

The other man grabbed for the dog, but then the escapee leapt to *his* head. Other workers ran up and the dog kept leaping from head

to head

to head

to head

to head and so forth.

You might think these acrobatics enough to fully occupy a dog's attention, but no, they are multitaskers at

She only got about twenty feet.

their core, and he finished chewing the stolen french fries. His first french fries ever, as it happens. The dog licked his lips and made a mental note that his favorite thing in the world was no longer kibble.

Inside the terminal, Mrs. Nutbush shrieked in horror at the sight of her Duüglitz dachshund escaping across the scalps of Piddleton's sweatiest luggage handlers. Heidy watched as the furred woman surged forward and body-slammed through the glass security doors. Airport alarms erupted, as did Mrs. Nutbush: "GET HIM! GET HIM! DON'T TOUCH THE TUFT!!" she yelled, arms out, hands waving, fur coat flapping. She got twenty feet before the first of a dozen security people tackled her, looking, Heidy thought, like the Notre Dame backfield piling atop a two-hundred-pound blue rodent.

Heidy gave a long, low whistle of awed admiration. "Some dog," she said aloud.

"A stray, no doubt. Mongrel!" snorted Mrs. Beaglehole. "Grubby, undisciplined mutts need a leash." As she mumbled this, she reached into her large purse and removed a dog leash. Heidy's eyes went large as the woman bent down toward Heidy's neck. She stopped, catching herself. "Old habit," she said, smiling that tight, lipless smile again. Mrs. Beaglehole picked up Heidy's bags and nudged Heidy out the front doors to a town car idling in front of the terminal, waiting to take her to the rest of her life.

FIVE

⇐ 737 ⇒

Heidy settled nervously into the backseat as the car pulled away onto the airport road. She never saw the renegade dachshund behind her on the tarmac leap into the cab of an electric airport cart and accidentally hit the accelerator with his bottom.

The little vehicle lurched forward and bounced below the belly of a parked airplane and on toward the runway. A dozen airport people chased the cart—a huge sign attached to its bumper read: **FOLLOW ME**. The dog wasn't actually steering, of course, but to his surprise, he found himself moving quickly away from Mrs. Nutbush, who was still flattened under the men on the tarmac. He kept his bottom pressed against the accelerator pedal and presumed, like a dog caught shredding and eating a designer sofa, that everything was going fine.

The **FOLLOW ME** vehicle entered the main runway from the side and directly across the path of a taxiing 737 airliner that had just landed from Dubuque. The little truck continued east across the grass toward the highway. The plane turned in the same direction and obediently followed close behind.

Meanwhile, Heidy sat unhappily in the back of the huge car moving down the airport perimeter road while Mrs. Beaglehole drove.

"Dear, sweet Heidy," the woman said. "We should probably discuss something before you see your uncle. The wonderful ladies of St. Egregious mentioned some . . . problems there that you had been involved with."

Heidy said nothing. Word must have gotten out about the flush reversals she'd arranged for the nuns' bathrooms. She stared at the back of the car seats. Little golden retrievers were carved into the leather.

"Your uncle Hamish's spirit isn't terribly well, dear. We'd hate for any . . . unnecessary stress to enter his life

right now." Heidy looked out the windows as the car moved away from the airport. She saw people on the sidewalk pointing back down the road behind them.

Heidy twisted around in her seat and looked out the rear window. The little electric airport cart swerved close behind their bumper, the dachshund's face peeking out over the hood. Close behind the **FOLLOW ME** cart rolled a 737 airliner and its obedient pilots moving down the country road.

Mrs. Beaglehole stared straight ahead in the front seat and continued: "Heidy, I'll just ask you straight out: Can we expect any problems ahead?"

Heidy stared behind her as the airliner's wings knocked down the power poles lining the road twenty yards back, sending sparks flying and exploding a small transformer box.

"No," she said.

On the weaving, bouncing electric cart, the dog spotted the girl peering at him through the car's rear window ahead of him. Amidst a troublesome day where nothing made sense, the girl's face was a lifeboat of familiarity. He leapt from the electric cart's accelerator pedal, stopping it cold. The airliner behind it slammed on its brakes in front of a Piggly Wiggly grocery store, which the passengers decided was the Piddleton Airport baggage claim.

The dachshund streaked up alongside Heidy's car, leapt onto the running board and scrambled up the rear door, through the open window, and into Heidy's open travel bag tucked next to her leg.

Panting hard, he looked up at the startled girl and said simply: *"I love french fries."*

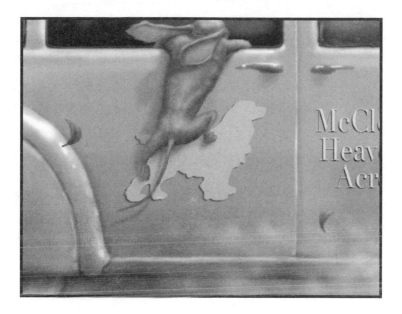

He honestly couldn't think of anything less stupid to say. But he thought something honest was called for. It was a pity that girls don't speak dog.

Heidy looked down in mute amazement.

Then with a single finger, Heidy gently, silently pushed the dachshund's muzzle into the bag and zipped it up.

SIX

- SNORT -

"I remember this place like a dream," said Heidy, allowing a smile. She leaned over Mrs. Beaglehole's shoulder and peered out the town car's front window at the extraordinary sight ahead of her. The car had turned off a country road and into a tunnel made of a dark canopy of great oak trees. As they emerged back into the sunlight, two twenty-foot-high Great Danes made of shrubbery stood sentinel on either side of the final entrance to

McCloud Heavenly Acres. The driveway pointed to the top of the highest hill for miles around, atop which stood the McCloud mansion, one of Heidy's faded memories from eight years before. She let out a low whistle, which made the renegade dachshund hiding in her bag stir. (Whistles are to dogs what a pricked thumb is to a vampire.) Heidy pushed her last taffy candy bar into the bag to quiet her stowaway.

"Something's different," said Heidy, still staring out the window. She saw rows and rows of empty kennels in the near distance. "The dogs are gone."

"Your uncle seemed to lose interest in dogs after your parents were . . . were . . ." Mrs. Beaglehole trailed off.

"You can just come out and say it," said Heidy. "Eaten by schnauzers."

Mrs. Beaglehole spun around and gave the smirking girl the evil cow eye. The woman was shocked at her coolness toward her parents. Why not coolness? Heidy had never known her family, really. Her memories of her parents were like dim figures peeking out from a thick fog. All she'd known for the last eight years was a girls' school in the freezing hills of Minnesota and platoons of behemoth penguins pretending to be nuns.

Mrs. Beaglehole continued: "Your uncle sold off all the beautiful dogs. All! So beautiful. Like tossing out Louis Vuitton handbags! *Snort!*" This was the first of many snorts of displeasure. Heidy read somewhere that water buffalo snort before they ram people. "Your uncle Hamish now mostly spends his time alone. Doesn't seem interested in much of anything. I arrived a few years ago to take care of things while he . . ." She snorted. "He's not well. Which is why he sent for you."

This time Heidy snorted.

She was going to demand the truth about her parents' deaths . . . and why her uncle had sent her away years ago . . . but changed her mind. She looked at the rows of empty kennels passing by. "There aren't any dogs left here AT ALL?"

Mrs. Beaglehole brightened visibly. "Why, yes, dear. Mine. That makes one!"

Heidy felt her bag move as the dachshund chewed his first banana taffy. *Two,* thought Heidy.

The car pulled up to the grand house's grand entrance, where Heidy's door was opened by a younger woman in a neat housekeeper's apron who didn't make Heidy think of cows at all. A quiet baby was slung tightly across her back in a sling. "Heidy McCloud! I'm Miss Violett. I look after your uncle's house. And the cooking. And my Bruno here, of course." She held up the baby's socked foot.

Mrs. Beaglehole snorted. "He looks like an Indian papoose, Violett."

Miss Violett took Heidy's hand and looked at her with a softness that she wasn't used to. "Your mother and I were good friends when we were girls. I used to play with her in this very house. And isn't it funny . . . now I'm back looking after her brother."

"Actually, Miss Violett, that is my job," injected Mrs. Beaglehole with an edge to her voice. "You see to lunch."

Mrs. Beaglehole climbed onto a step leading to the front door, so that she was slightly higher than either of them. "Come along, your uncle is waiting to see you. You're off a button with your sweater, dear."

Heidy followed Mrs. Beaglehole into the entry. She gasped. Dark-paneled walls soared to a ceiling three stories above her. Straight ahead, a grand staircase curved upward into darkness. In fact, the entire house was dark. But that's not what made the girl stop and stare.

The dogs. Ghosts of McCloud family purebreds. The walls were covered with them. In huge paintings eight feet tall, they sat rigid and regal, as if stunned into bewildered awe by the glory of their own fabulousness.

A Bolivian flat-nosed spittin' spaniel. An orange-crested Dutch baby dusenstruegal. A Chinese kissin' tellin' terrier. Many more, far more exotic. Heidy let out another long, low whistle.

Which again made the dachshund hiding inside the bag across her shoulder stop chewing the taffy and reflexively blurt out: *"What! Hello! I'm here! My tongue ith thtuck to the woof of my mowth."*

He said this in dog, of course, and it emerged as a garbled yip. Heidy heard it and tried to cover it up by shuffling a large chair next to her. Mrs. Beaglehole glanced about. "Moles," she sniffed.

There was another set of ears nearby, however, far less easily fooled. A large poodle with a red bow came tearing in from the kitchen, barking maniacally. *"I HEARD THAT! WHO WAS THAT!?"* he yelled.

Mrs. Beaglehole spun around and threw her arms wide. "There's my darling champion to be! Heidy, THIS is Cassius."

Heidy stared at the pathetic creature. Beachball-size

explosions of fuzzy hair erupted like creeping blobs of attacking white broccoli across the entirety of the starved beast's shaved skeleton. "Is he going to die?" asked Heidy.

"On the contrary. He's going to win Westminster one day," said Mrs. Beaglehole, reaching down through miles of poodle fur and fluffing it up to an even more terrifying extent.

Cassius turned to Mrs. Beaglehole with a lick to her nose. She thrust out a hand to stop him. "Tut! No lickies, Cassius! You *know* only on my feet and before bath time!"

"I shall count the minutes until paradise, madam,"

mumbled the poodle, rolling his eyes. He looked around the room. He'd heard a yip. He knew a yip when he heard one, and it wasn't a stupid yard mole. He ate them all the time and they never yipped.

Unless, he thought, you started at the tail and went veeeery slow.

SEVEN

— POOFED —

"Heidy! Come to me, Niece!" a man's voice said from the darkness above the stairs. The girl froze. Then she moved to the source of the voice as commanded, climbing the stairs slowly. She peered into a vast, dark room.

"You got my letters?" asked the voice of Uncle Hamish somewhere in the black depths of a huge chair. Cassius stood nearby, eyes glowing like embers.

"Yep. Got 'em," said Heidy, standing in the doorway, unsmiling.

"You look like your mother, Heidy," said Hamish.

"Well, that's a relief, Uncle. People start looking like their dogs after enough time." She stared at her uncle. "It's been eight years. I figured I might start looking like the nuns."

Hamish was silent for a moment. "I know you're angry, Heidy," he finally said.

He suddenly stood up into the firelight. He was still in his pajamas, and his hair was long and mussed. "I knew how to sight the slightest detour in the backbone of a Pookishtan dingle hound from two hundred feet. I could massage out the kinks from the curls of a crested Capetown kinkapoodle. I knew how to nurse twenty puppies with twenty bottles with two hands and another five with my feet! Twenty!"

Hamish pointed at Heidy. "But I couldn't braid a six-year-old girl's ponytail."

"I do my own braiding," said Heidy, not buying it for a second.

He ran a hand through his hair. "I'm sorry. Parenting you would've made as much sense as Cassius here herding sheep."

"The horror," said Cassius. *"The grass stains."*

Heidy felt the bag on her shoulder move. The dachshund wanted out. *I do too,* thought Heidy.

Hamish collapsed back into his huge chair and put his face in his hands. He spoke quietly this time. "It . . . it was *me* who dreamed of finding a champion Tibetan yak nibbler hound. It was *my* dream. But when the hot air balloon went down in the storm over the Himalayan mountains, it wasn't me in it. It was your parents. I had sent them instead." He looked up at the little girl. "Me. It should have been me."

Hamish looked empty. The dogs in the paintings seemed to peer down at the rumpled man with cold judgment.

"I think I died too, Heidy. This was no longer a place for life. Or show dogs. Or little girls."

He collected himself and stood again. "But you're older now. There's something I want you to see."

Hamish moved unsteadily toward the towering window, covered with a heavy curtain tapestry. "All I want now . . . is for you to stay. All this . . . McCloud Heavenly Acres will be yours. Soon. It's time you made it so. This house. This world. *Yours.*"

"Mine?" sputtered Heidy.

She suddenly noticed Mrs. Beaglehole standing in one of the room's dark corners, listening and watching her carefully, quietly. Cassius sat next to her, doing the same. The huge poodle rose and moved to Heidy, where he slipped his long bony nose into her hand dangling at her side so that her fingers cradled his chin. He looked up at her with coal black eyes. *"No. Ours,"* said Cassius.

44

She pulled her hand away.

Hamish drew back the window curtains, flooding the room with dazzling sunlight. Heidy looked out the window and gasped.

The entire population of Piddleton was in the backyard. Cars covered the nearby hills, brightly striped tents sat amidst the verdant gardens and people milled about the sprawling lawn in their finest Sunday clothes. The women were festooned in sparkling bracelets and astonishingly large hats in the shape of inverted serving bowls. Men sported two-toned shoes and pressed cream trousers. Children chased each other and dropped ice cream onto lace-trimmed skirts.

And each gloved hand held a leash, at the end of which was a strutting hound of traffic-stopping beauty . . . of brushed and curled and poofed fur glistening like woven gold . . . and noses and backbones aligned more perfectly than the pyramids of Egypt. The ancient oaks overhead seemed almost to bow at the sight of so much naked dog glamour passing below them.

The pampered paws moved toward a central clearing on the lawn, around which hundreds of white folding chairs awaited the pressed linen bottoms of their proud owners. A woman with a clipboard stood waving in the center.

"It's a dog show," said Heidy, staring below, guessing correctly that it wasn't the Spring Tractor Pull.

"The Piddleton Open," said her uncle, without zeal.

"Held here at McCloud Heavenly Acres every year for the past hundred. Go down there and dip in your toes, Niece. It's your new pond."

"Mine?" asked Heidy again, eyes wide, incredulous. She looked down into the rolling ocean of flowered hats and perfumed spaniels as she would lava. "Are you coming with me, Uncle?" She looked up to see that she was alone. "Uncle?" she whispered into the room's darkness. There was only silence. The firelight flickered on the faces of the dogs in the paintings staring down, now at her.

EIGHT

– $180,000 –

Out! There's that word again, popping into her head for the second time today, pressing on the inside of her skull as she hurried through the front door toward the McCloud Heavenly Acres gate. *Out! OUT!*

Now this word too: *AWAY!*

Also these: *Go! Now! Quick! Before anyone pulls you back into this cuckoo land of demented dog dips!*

She passed Violett carrying a tray of champagne glasses

toward the backyard, baby Bruno strapped happily across her back. "Heidy! Where are you going?"

"Fiji!"

She kept moving, then suddenly stopped at the gate, remembering the dachshund bouncing around in her bag. She pulled the dog out and set him on the lawn at the edge of the woods, where he wobbled a bit as he looked up at her.

"That was fun!" he said. *"What's next, pardner?"*

"Shh! Go! You're liberated. Join a pack of wolves!"

He looked at her squarely*: "I have to tell you: banana taffy is my new favorite thing."*

Heidy began backing away, but the little dog followed.

"No! Go! GO!!" she yelled. "They don't allow dogs in Fiji! They pee on the coconuts!" This was a guess. Her tone turned angry: "Go very far away. I'm doing the same."

The dachshund kept following. Heidy put her face down to his and was about to scream louder when he licked the underside of her nose.

She froze at this unexpected attack.

A familiar shriek from behind made her jump. She turned to see Mrs. Nutbush from the airport—still in her blue fur coat—run in and scoop up the dachshund, holding it above her head. "MY LOST LITTLE DUÜGLITZ TUFT!! Where have you BEEN, naughty boy!"

The dog looked as if it was about to be eaten. Which, in a sense, it was.

Heidy looked down the road to freedom. Then she looked back at Mrs. Nutbush, terrified dog in hand.

"Arrrgghhh . . ." muttered Heidy under her breath as she pulled the little dog from the woman's grasp, giving him the sternest angry-nun look that she could muster. "Naughty boy is right! Always chasing big . . . blue . . ." She looked at Mrs. Nutbush. ". . . critters."

"Well, n-n-now, who are you and why do you have my Duüglitz-tufted Austrian red dachshund?" stammered the flustered woman, reaching for the shaking animal. Heidy backed away.

"I'm Heidy McCloud. And this is . . . this is, uh . . ."

She needed a name. Her imagination failed her:

"Sam. My dog Sam."

"Sam? SAM?" repeated Mrs. Nutbush, suspicious.

"Yes! Good ol' Sam . . . *the Lion.*" An entirely perfect name, Sam the Lion. Heidy looked down at Sam and gave him a little eyebrow flash, which is more a warning than a wink, meaning: We're both in it up to our butts now, pal.

Sam looked back at her in panic. *"Do NOT hand me back to the blue and hairy woman,"* he said. *"I will throw up taffy and fries on her."*

Mrs. Nutbush narrowed her eyes and leaned in to Heidy. "I think the police might like to know why a discarded snot-nosed orphaned McCloud has a one-of-a-kind $180,000 *Duüglitz* dachshund," she sneered.

Heidy's eyes popped. $180,000?

She looked down at Sam. "You poop rubies?"

"WHY WOULD YOU HAVE SUCH A DOG?!" demanded Mrs. Nutbush.

Good question.

Heidy opened her mouth. Nothing.

"It was a gift from her uncle," said a voice from behind. It was Miss Violett, holding a punch bowl containing a humming baby Bruno. "Goodness, no reason to involve the police with an honest misunderstanding, Mrs. Nutbush," she said as she laid a gentle hand atop Heidy's strewn hair and stared carefully into the girl's surprised face. "You're late, Miss McCloud. The competition is about to start. Take . . . Sam the Lion there and hurry on to register."

Heidy, too confused to argue, moved back through the gate, past the huge dog-shaped bushes and toward the house. She looked back at Miss Violett, who gave her an eyebrow flash.

Nobody before had given *her* an eyebrow flash.

A smiling Violett turned to a shocked Mrs. Nutbush. Violett daubed her eyes with a corner of her apron. "Heidy and Sam's first show! A big moment for all of us." *Sniff.*

Mrs. Nutbush snorted a suspicious snort, pushed past Violett and stomped after the girl holding her $180,000 Duüglitz dachshund.

Heidy walked as if in a trance . . . back toward the dreadful place that she had just run from. Sinister cosmic forces beyond her understanding had seized her life, she figured. All she could do was put one foot in front of the other and not fall over.

Carrying Sam and his Duüglitz-tuft-whatever thing, she stumbled toward the jostling crowd and their trash-can-lid hats and their hydraulic bosoms and their powdered, poof-erized dogs and the gathering realization that this was going to be the end of her life.

She found herself at the end of a long line of fancy people with fancy dogs at the center of the McCloud Heavenly Acres back lawn. She stood frozen in dazed terror, gripping Sam close to her chest. Upside down.

She was in a dog show. The horror.

The competition was about done. Heidy became dimly aware of people clapping and cheering. She looked up to see a beaming Mrs. Beaglehole getting back in line after showing the dazzling, showstopping Cassius. The people in the surrounding lawn chairs clapped loudly while Mrs. Beaglehole smiled triumphantly and made a little bow to the crowd. The big poodle had won the Piddleton best in show for the past three years. He would grease this one, and Mrs. Beaglehole knew it.

The world championship Westminster show in New York City lay in the future. Cassius would win best in show.

51

The most beautiful dog on the planet. They *both* knew this.

"Wait a minute, ladies and gentlemen," announced a lady with a microphone and clipboard at the center of the lawn. "A last-minute entry has been added. It's . . . oh, what a lovely surprise . . . Heidy McCloud, Hamish McCloud's niece! And her Austrian red dachshund . . . Ham the Lion."

"Sam," corrected Heidy in the tiniest whisper.

The crowd went dead silent.

A shocked Mrs. Beaglehole and Cassius spun their heads to stare at her at the end of the line.

Then a frantic, low murmuring raced throughout the crowd: "The little orphan McCloud girl!" "A McCloud hasn't shown up at their own dog show for ten years!" "She looks like her mother." "They say at school she set the nuns' toilets to flush in reverse!"

Heidy heard all of this, which made her mortification complete. She wondered if the others could hear the pounding of her heart.

"Miss McCloud and Sam the Lion!" said the woman in the center, gesturing toward Heidy. "The judges await."

Heidy stared. The judges awaited what? Here was the dog in her hands. What else did they need?

The clipboard woman gestured to her to do something.

What? What did people do at dog shows? Hundreds of eyes were on her as her panic slipped into action, and she instantly went with her best guess. She put Sam on the ground.

Then she began to dance.

She'd been good at dancing, and her freestyle was legendary among the students at St. Egregious. So she played Elvis's "Hound Dog" in her head, closed her eyes and let it all fly.

Sam stared up at Heidy's windmilling arms and legs and wondered if this simply was what all human beings suddenly did around noon every day.

So he began to dance as well. Hopping. Twirling. Bouncing. Heidy smiled. He looked like he was on a hot skillet.

Then Sam noticed Mrs. Nutbush. She was in the crowd and moving closer, dead set, he figured, on eating him. So Sam did what worked before and shot up Heidy's legs to find high ground. In this case, to the top of her head.

The tittering began. Tittering is polite laughter that never stays polite. Eventually, all three hundred dog lovers were spewing champagne punch through their noses in open hysterics.

Heidy only danced harder, while Sam hung on. He found himself nose to nose with the judge.

Her eyes went to the top of his head.

The judge stopped laughing.

"The Duüglitz tuft!" she said in an awed whisper normally saved for matters of religion or premium gossip.

Her mouth dropped. Then slowly, one by one, Piddleton's fanciest citizens began murmuring the same thing: "The Duüglitz . . . *the Duüglitz . . . !*"

And one by one, they stood in solemn reverence. As if the pope himself had suddenly alighted upon Heidy McCloud's head.

The most supernaturally beautiful dog that any had ever seen was before them. Sam's perfect proportions, crowned with his tuft born of almost inconceivably careful breeding, was almost more than many could take. Flemmie Croup in the back fainted and needed slapping.

For a moment, Heidy thought that her dancing had won the crowd over . . . but then realized that all eyes were on Sam.

She looked up at her uncle's window. The curtains were parted enough for her to see that his face peered down. Suddenly it was gone.

The judge approached and handed Heidy a large silver trophy cup while people clapped. Heidy had never won anything in her life other than time-outs in the closet from nuns.

She looked around at the grinning, cheering strangers . . . who suddenly didn't seem so strange anymore.

The judge tied a blue ribbon around Sam's neck and smiled at the dog. Sam grinned back. *"I love banana taffy,"* he said.

Sam began to dance as well.
Hopping. Twirling. Bouncing.

NINE

- GOPHER -

The crowd roared their approval and then, very suddenly, hushed to silence. They parted as if somebody important was moving through. More murmuring: "It's Hamish McCloud!" "Hidden for all these years!" "He's come out!"

Heidy's uncle, still in his robe and pajamas, moved unsteadily toward her, wincing in the noon light, as would a prisoner emerging from a dark prison cell. He looked at

Heidy, then at Sam. He plucked the dog from her head and stretched out his long torso, examining his ears, nose, toes, fur and finally the wonderful tuft. He looked back down at Heidy.

"Where did you get him, Niece?"

The crowd stared. Heidy saw Miss Violett standing off to the side with a plate of little sandwiches. She smiled sadly at Heidy and didn't give her an eyebrow flash.

Heidy looked up at Hamish and then at Sam. "He just . . . dropped into my life."

"Is he yours?" asked Hamish.

"NO!" thundered another voice. The crowd parted yet again, revealing Mrs. Nutbush in her blue fur, stomping toward them across the lawn, waving a shipping receipt. Her pointy heels suddenly sank into a mushy patch in the grass and she stopped, struggling to pull free.

Heidy dropped a horrified Sam to the ground. "RUN!" she screamed. "GO! RUN FREE! LIVE IN THE FOREST LIKE A GNOME!"

Sam didn't run. It had been a confusing day, but one thing was very, very clear: He didn't want to live like a gnome. He wanted only one thing now. Looking up at Heidy, he knew exactly what it was.

Mrs. Nutbush wobbled closer toward Sam, arms reaching out, eyes ablaze, fur gyrating and flying.

Enough is enough, thought Sam the Lion. *Time for action.*

He turned to face all the show dogs lined up beside him. He yelled one word, very loud and very clear.

The other dogs pricked their ears. There are exactly four words that are genetically guaranteed to turn a gaggle of pampered lapdogs into a mob of killers. "Federal. Express. Guy." are three.

The fourth is the word that Sam now said.

"Gopher."

At the sound of it, the dogs spun their heads and spotted a furry blue rodent of monstrous proportions.

Mrs. Nutbush froze five yards from Sam. Four dozen of Piddleton's finest purebreds blocked her way, noses flaring.

Mrs. Nutbush flared her own nostrils right back at them.

Sam uttered the magic word again:

"*Gopher!*"

"*GOPHER!*" they repeated like a chant. "*GOPHER! GOPHER!*"

Good-bye.

The human owners dove to avoid the explosion of their howling, barking darlings galloping across the lawn, leashes ripped from their gloved hands. Led by a snapping, saliva-spewing shih tzu named Mr. Tinkles, the fifty-two elegant

show dogs chased a screaming Mrs. Nutbush and her blue gopher fur coat through the orange meringue on the dessert table, under the coffee cart and directly through the Heavenly Acres reflecting pond.

Now, this is a shocking and violent part of the story, and there's no need to dwell on the details. All that anyone needs to know is that by the time the Piddleton police department removed Mrs. Nutbush from the empty Heavenly Acres dog kennel into which she had dived, she was mostly naked but unhurt. Her blue fur coat, however, would be aggravating the delicate bowels of Piddleton's parlor dogs for weeks to come.

Hamish McCloud and Heidy watched as a babbling, blanket-wrapped Mrs. Nutbush was strapped to a gurney and driven away in an ambulance. Her car was towed by the police captain, who turned to Heidy and said that it might take some time until the woman recovered from her emotional collapse. Would Heidy mind looking after Mrs. Nutbush's new Austrian red Duüglitz dachshund? . . . And give him a home?

Heidy looked at Sam, who looked back at her. She gave him a little eyebrow flash.

She thought he gave her one back.

"Sure," said Heidy quietly.

Now there's a word, thought Heidy. *Home.* Hamish put an arm across her shoulders, and they both turned to walk back toward her new one.

TEN

‐ MURDER ‐

Heidy slept in a room by herself for the first time since she could remember. No other girls. No nuns. No locked doors.

Only one dachshund curled up in the crook of her knees. A first for both.

She slept, exhausted from both the day and the dizzying reality that her life had turned inside out, becoming an object that she could at least begin to see as something having a recognizable shape. Beyond that, all bets were off.

Sam couldn't sleep himself. He had a human of his own, he was lying in the bend of her knees and they were all on this marvelous thing called a bed. Who could sleep?

He looked at the slumbering girl, her butt arched toward the ceiling, arms bent in a pretzel below her stomach and saliva pooling slightly on the pillow below her open mouth, exhaling wheezing half snortles unique to exhausted, happy fourteen-year-olds.

They're so cute when they're sleeping, he said to himself. *I'm definitely keeping her.*

Eager to explore the huge house, Sam jumped to the floor and wandered out of the room and into the upstairs hallway, which seemed to stretch for miles. Light glowed around a half-open door at the distant end. He loped toward it, curious who in this wonderful place would be up so late.

With a long nose, Sam pushed the door open. Uncle Hamish looked up from his desk, wireless spectacles balanced on the end of his nose. His face stretched into a beaming smile.

"Sam the Lion! Our champion! Come here, lad, and let me have a close look at you . . . and that marvelous *tuft*!" Hamish held his hands out wide, welcoming, warm.

Sam walked carefully toward the man in the pajamas. Hamish swept the dog up into his large hands and held him toward the lamp. With quiet awe, he moved his eyes over the perfect lines of Sam's profile. "A once-in-a-lifetime masterpiece," Hamish murmured.

"Thanks," said Sam, licking Hamish under the nose.

Hamish looked startled. For a moment he considered returning the kiss but instead ran a hand across the top of the Duúglitz tuft, down Sam's neck and across the length of his lanky back. "You and I are going to be great friends," said Hamish. "And you are going to go great places."

Hamish cradled Sam across his arm and walked to the open French doors looking out over the estate and the rolling hills glowing a milky blue below an autumn Vermont moon. He leaned his knees against the stone railing high above the ground, holding Sam up and out so he too could see to the horizon. "The McClouds are back, Sam. You're going to be the champion of the world, dear boy. *My* champion."

Sam hadn't the slightest clue what that meant. But he knew the hands that held him firmly and that stroked his head with warmth and strength were not unkind. And he liked it.

But there was someone else in the shadows of the great room who had heard these words but did not like any part of them.

Cassius stepped forward out of the shadows of an alcove, the flickering firelight dancing across lips curled up with rage. His teeth—polished to a glistening brilliance with Dr. Doogie's Doggy Dental Powder—sparkled. His eyes glowed with more than malice.

Murder.

"There is only one champion in this family," whispered the huge poodle as he crept toward the back of Hamish, still holding Sam into the chilly sky against the low stone railing. *"And it is not a ridiculous frankfurter on feet with a bit of laundry lint on his head."*

He stopped two yards from Hamish and Sam, facing the sky, breathing heavily, his breath misting from the cool air of the open window. A single impact at the man's shoulder blades would send him and this new creature toward the stone porch far below. He hesitated for only one reason:

This was going to scuff his nails.

Still. Sacrifices had to be made.

Cassius bent his rear legs, preparing to spring.

Heidy awoke in her huge room, thirsty. She reached for Sam behind her knees. Not there.

She padded in bare feet out of the room and into the hall, whispering Sam's name. So many rooms.

Heidy saw light at the end of the hall in her uncle's study. She moved toward it, a faint feeling of unease urging her feet toward the light.

"Hot cocoa?" said Mrs. Beaglehole, stepping out from the hall's darkness and in front of Heidy, scaring her. The large woman held a glass in front of the girl.

She was blocking her.

Heidy felt the hair on her neck rise.

"Poor dear," said Mrs. Beaglehole. "You can't sleep after the excitement today. This will help."

"Have you seen Sam?" asked Heidy, suddenly suspicious and ignoring the glass.

"Why, no. But I'm sure he's near. Go back to bed and I'll look, dear."

Heidy nudged the big woman aside and moved toward her uncle's door. Reaching it, she flipped on the light switch, bathing the room in brilliance. Outside the French window on the veranda, Hamish spun around, Sam in his arms. He looked down to see Cassius behind him, crouched, ears down.

Cassius froze . . . then dropped to the floor, feigning a yawn to mask his murderous rage.

"Heidy. It's so late," said her uncle, surprised.

Heidy stood in the study doorway, blinking in the light. "Sam was gone. I didn't know where he went."

Mrs. Beaglehole and a pale Miss Violett came up behind Heidy.

"We do now," Mrs. Beaglehole said with an odd, dark smile. She held up baby Bruno's knitted sweater.

It had been violently shredded by sharp teeth.

ELEVEN

— BEAST —

Several months had stripped the trees of all their color, and winter was descending.

The school bus stopped at the gates of the McCloud estate. The door swung open while a dozen faces pushed up against the windows, staring, waiting, expectant.

Inside, the bus driver turned around to face Heidy, sitting three rows back. The girl looked terrified. The bus driver raised an eyebrow: *Out.*

Heidy took her backpack and held it to her chest. Like a shield. She stepped hesitantly down the steps and onto the dirt driveway, looking around nervously. She looked up at the kids staring down at her from the windows, waiting for something to happen.

Heidy moved toward the house slowly, trying not to make any sounds on the gravel with her shoes. She watched the afternoon shadows of the shrubbery and gate for any sign of movement. The kids' eyes in the bus did the same.

The driver quickly shut the door . . . but didn't drive off. She too stared out with wide eyes. Watching. Waiting. Looking.

Heidy glanced up at the looming topiary bushes carved into the shape of huge dogs and shuddered, but not from the growing chill of the late autumn. No, it was from fear of the thing that was surely near.

The beast.

It waited for her.

Somewhere close.

It *watched*.

Heidy knew, as did the others, that it would soon attack. Without mercy.

Heidy spun. A figure leapt toward her neck from the nose of the huge dog bush overhead.

The kids in the bus screamed, "RUN!"

She did. The beast hit the ground behind her and she could hear its foul, murderous breath exhale. Heidy slipped on the gravel, landing painfully on one knee, her backpack slipping off. She left it behind and made for the safety of the house a hundred yards up the hill.

The beast followed, snapping at her heels, teeth flashing, voice screaming in a primordial howl.

The kids screamed again and pounded the bus's windows.

She wasn't going to make it.

As usual.

The beast leapt, its claws digging deep into her argyle sweater. Heidy dropped from the impact, hitting the grassy berm beside the drive. Rolling onto her back, she fought off the snapping jaws while the horrified audience in the bus continued to scream.

The beast's terrible mouth reached Heidy's neck and she surrendered to the inevitable, lying back against the ground while his tongue did what it always did at 3:40 P.M. every school day and lathered the lower part of her nose with dog saliva.

The kids in the bus shifted from screaming to cheering. Michael Green turned to Shayla Morphy with a look of triumph: "She made it to the third sprinkler head. *She's getting better!*"

The bus drove away, the voices of the kids fading.

Heidy lay on her back in the cold grass, Sam sprawled across her chest, front feet on either side of her neck, licking above her top lip.

"Sam the Lion. Missed me?" asked Heidy.

"Did," said Sam.

"You wonder how my day was? Ah. Well. Esther Newberg asked to borrow my gym locker because she'd forgotten her combination and then she stole my gym underwear, wrote my name all over it in big letters and pulled it over a helium balloon and sent it up over the school assembly while we sang the national anthem."

"I'm so sorry."

"This is why I like dogs," Heidy said.

"Exactly. We don't fly panties."

"How was your day?" she asked Sam.

"Busy. Slept. Ate a potato bug."

"You didn't rip up any more of baby Bruno's clothes?"

"I told you," sighed Sam. *"That wasn't me."*

"You didn't puncture his baby bottle with your teeth? Or leave gnawing marks on his crib yesterday?"

"Nor did I eat the gardener."

"Uncle doesn't know what to think. Miss Violett thinks it's Cassius. Mrs. Beaglehole told Uncle that it must have been you. She wanted to check your gums for splinters."

"Anyone check Beaglehole's gums?" asked Sam.

Heidy studied Sam's eyes, not his teeth. She laid her head back down and stared up at the gathering clouds. A

snowflake landed on her nose. "You just wouldn't do those things. I know it. You couldn't hurt anyone."

"I feel bad enough about the potato bug."

Heidy stroked Sam's head, kissed him on his forehead and then gently pushed his head down so his long nose lay under her ear, where she could feel his breath on her neck, warm, moist, safe. She laid both her hands across his back as if someone were about to pluck him from her grasp. She felt his chest rise and fall with his breathing. Now snoring.

She couldn't help but match her breaths with his. They breathed as one.

And slept.

From the second-story window of Mrs. Beaglehole's

room, Cassius sat staring down at Heidy below with Sam sprawled across her neck. One thought circulated through his beautiful head: *That should be me.*

Cassius looked up into the sky while the winter's first good whopper of a storm began to move in, the darkness descending across the rolling hills. A gathering gale pushed frozen rain bouncing off windowpanes, sounding like needles falling on glass. The poodle's black eyes became even blacker.

It is time, he thought.

TWELVE

– SCREAMS –

As always, Sam woke up for his 5:55 A.M. pee. He uncurled from Heidy's inner knee, slipped from her bed and padded down the stairs and outside through the kitchen dog door.

Sam stood on the top step and sniffed with distaste the freezing dawn gloom beyond the porch overhang. Winter's first snow was falling fast and thick. *"How uninviting,"* he said. He turned and looked at the rows of potted petunias that Uncle Hamish kept safely out of the weather, near the warmth of the house.

He lifted his leg and watered the one on the far right. It looked the most needy.

Returning inside to the kitchen, he was surprised to see Cassius, who normally slept until noon in his curlers. The poodle trotted up to him with a look of deep concern on his face.

"There's a crisis, dear Sam. Poor baby Bruno is missing from his crib!"

"Missing?" said Sam. *"He can't even crawl. Do human babies fly?"*

"I fear he's been taken. Go, please check the eastern ridge. I thought I saw a dark figure moving up there through the blizzard. You're better in the snow than me. My fur catches the flakes like Velcro and I freeze into a dogsicle. I'll wake the others."

"Right!"

Sam sprang with urgency. He turned and tore back through the kitchen dog door, into the driving snow and toward the eastern ridge beyond the aspen grove. He was forced to bound like a rabbit, his short legs struggling in the deepening drifts. He was past the aspens and close to the crest of the ridge before it even occurred to him how preposterous a thing it was that Cassius had just said. Come to think of it, Cassius was built perfectly for bounding around in a Vermont blizzard—plenty of fluff for insulation and pole-like legs.

If anyone was suited for becoming a dogsicle in the snow, it was Sam, not Cassius.

Just as this bit of obviousness was breaking through the early-morning fog of his still-sleepy brain, he saw the baby.

As soon as Sam left the house, Cassius turned and loped back behind the kitchen to the cook's quarters. He entered Miss Violett's room and stopped. He could hear the measured breaths of the woman and confirmed that she was still asleep. He continued into the adjoining small sewing room that had recently been turned into a nursery for Bruno. He looked at the crib, its front wall hanging down, exposing the empty interior. His chew marks were all around the clasp. Bruno's blankets were ripped apart and strewn about the room just as Cassius had left them a few moments before.

Cassius decided the scene needed a coup de grace . . . a final colorful brushstroke to the masterpiece.

The poodle knelt down and took his right paw into his mouth. He hooked his sharpest tooth between the tough pads and sank it deep into the softer pink flesh below . . . just enough to break the surface. Then he rose on his hind legs until his front feet lay on the baby's bedding. He held his paw over the white linen adorned with colorful cartoon characters . . . and carefully let three bright red drops of his own blood fall just to the side of a stuffed bear's head.

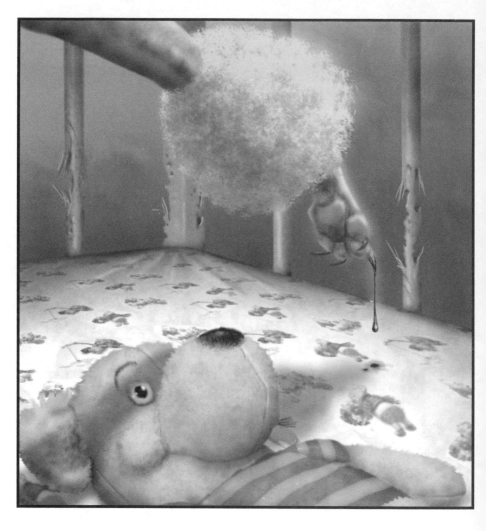

Cassius stepped back, satisfied. He looked toward the still-sleeping Miss Violett in the adjoining room. He set his feet wide, arched his back, adopted a convincing expression of alarm on his bony face . . . and began barking.

Miss Violett's screams started very soon after.

THIRTEEN

- FIRED -

At the top of the eastern ridge, Sam looked down through the blowing snow at the bundle of blankets tucked into a small blueberry bush. With a long nose, he prodded the folds until Bruno's little face emerged. The baby yawned, stretched and looked up at Sam. He smiled as the snow tickled his nose.

Sam was confused. But only for a second, for his own nose had picked up a familiar scent as he pushed the blanket open, a scent easily identified in a house with only two dogs.

Cassius.

His mouth. His saliva. His *hair spray.*

The morning fog suddenly cleared in the dachshund's now-racing brain. The fur along his backbone stood up as the final scent he sniffed overwhelmed his senses:

Danger.

What Sam didn't sense at that moment was that the threat wasn't to baby Bruno . . . but to himself.

Sam pulled the blanket folds back over the face of the giggling Bruno, grasped the material and pulled the heavy bundle from the bush and onto the soft snow.

He heard Cassius barking.

Turning at the sound, he saw Miss Violett in the distance stumbling up the ridge and through the storm, toward them. Behind her came Uncle Hamish and Heidy— everyone in their nightclothes despite the cold.

But Cassius was ahead of them all, barking, baying. He would reach Sam and the baby in seconds. One thought crowded out all others in a dachshund brain still churning, trying to make sense of it all:

Keep the baby away from Cassius.

Sam spun and ran down the opposite side of the ridge, his neck muscles bulging as he struggled to keep his head high, the bundled baby dangling under his mouth.

Miss Violett saw this and screamed again. Behind her,

Heidy and her uncle pushed through the snow with frantic urgency. "SAM! WHAT ARE YOU DOING? SAM!!" screamed Heidy, her voice hysterical and breaking from a swirling mix of confusion and fear.

Sam reached a low stone wall, which blocked further retreat. He set baby Bruno carefully against the wall and turned to face the quickly closing Cassius. Violett, Hamish and Heidy reached the top of the ridge and looked down on the two dogs, now facing off.

Sam was outmatched and he knew it. The poodle was five times his size and weight. The little dog planted his feet wide, placing himself between Cassius and the child. He put his head low. *"I don't understand any of this,"* Sam said. *"But I know you're not touching the baby again."*

"Yes," said Cassius, slowly, evenly. *"I am."*

Sam locked terrified eyes at Cassius, his lips curling high in anger for the first time in his brief life. He spat forth a vicious snarl, punctuated by barks and the snapping of his teeth that echoed through the small valley.

And it was here, in a distant icy meadow below a black sky at the dawn of a terrible day, that Sam would demonstrate the other thing besides kisses that dogs uniquely offer people willingly:

Their lives.

But the people watching from the ridge above that day didn't see this. All they saw was a crazed, probably very ill dachshund intent on killing an infant and threatening anyone that would stop him.

Cassius stepped toward Sam, who made a lunge at the big dog before spinning around to move back toward baby Bruno, where he would make his last stand.

This is when Uncle Hamish raised his rifle and fired.

FOURTEEN

— DESCENT —

Sam lay on his side in the snow and was even more unsure about what was happening than he'd been just seconds before. He knew there was a searing pain across the top of his head but didn't know that it was from a bullet that had grazed his skull, leaving an ugly gash oozing the scent of blood: a first for the dachshund.

He couldn't move, but his vision cleared and he could see Heidy clawing through the snow trying to get to him.

He watched Uncle Hamish still in pajamas drop the gun and tackle her just as she reached him, Heidy's hair tangled and her mouth open. Sam's ears were ringing too loud to hear that she was screaming.

To Sam's relief, Miss Violett picked up her baby and frantically tore off the blanket that still wrapped him. She and Hamish scanned the naked child and seemed reassured by what they saw. Little Bruno smiled up at his mother as if it was a game.

Sam could see Heidy, crouched on her knees and crying, staring at him but not moving closer.

"Don't worry, Heidy," said Sam quietly. *"Everything is okay. The baby's safe. Why aren't you coming to me?"*

Then he saw Cassius move close to Miss Violett, now on her knees as well, holding baby Bruno close. Cassius stared at Sam carefully while he pushed his mouth in close to the bundled baby.

Closer.

"No!" exploded Sam. *"Stop him! STOP HIM! DON'T YOU ALL SEE? CASSIUS WILL KILL HIM!"*

Sam didn't realize that he was snapping his jaws again, lips curled into a frenzied rage. Instincts—cold and unsparing—ruled his actions now, and his feet clawed the snow wildly in a desperate attempt to get between Cassius and Bruno once more.

The others backed away from the writhing, snarling little dog lying in the snow, now red with his blood. Uncle Hamish pushed away a sobbing Heidy with an arm across the girl's chest. Then Sam watched in a shocked daze of incomprehension as Hamish raised his rifle again. He pointed it directly at him.

Sam closed his eyes and said simply, quietly:

"Heidy."

But Heidy had leapt at her uncle and knocked the muzzle toward the ground. Sam's hearing had returned enough to hear her scream, "NO, UNCLE!" Sam watched the man crouch before Heidy on her knees and hold her shoulders. He looked into the girl's horrified eyes and spoke something slowly, carefully. Sam could only hear a few words: "Can't touch him," "very sick" and "must be destroyed."

The girl collapsed into her uncle's arms, shaking with sobs. He held her. Maybe for the first time. Violett reached out and laid a hand on the girl's back while she held Bruno close.

Sam's mind swam in confusion, the pain from the bullet pushed to the background. He tried to stand, to reach Heidy, to tell her that everything was okay, to lick the underpart of her nose, to kiss her.

But he couldn't.

Instead he felt himself being wrapped in a cloth, maybe a bathrobe. Uncle Hamish carried him, but not in the direction of the house with the others. They were going over the stone wall, toward the aspen forest. Sam caught a final fleeting glimpse of Heidy being pulled up the hill toward the house by Miss Violett. The girl kept turning back to look at Sam. Cassius moved next to her, leaning in. Protectively. Possessively. Sam looked farther up the ridge and saw Mrs. Beaglehole standing serenely, watching it all without emotion.

As Hamish carried a limp and increasingly faint Sam into the forest, Sam heard the last of Heidy's voice—halting and desperate—calling to him, blending with the growing howl of the wind.

"Forgive me," she was yelling.

Then blackness descended on Sam's world.

Uncle Hamish raised his rifle and fired.

FIFTEEN

– MEN –

Sam opened his eyes to see Hamish looking down at him with a tortured look. He lay in snow between two large roots extending from a huge fig tree. His head hurt less now, but he still couldn't stand up.

Hamish held his rifle to his chest, his fingers tightening on the stock, turning white from the cold. He swung the barrel toward the dachshund and held it there, his hands shaking. With the other hand he wiped the falling snow from his eyes awkwardly.

"I don't understand what has happened," said Sam weakly. *"Why is everyone afraid of me?"*

Hamish listened to the faint sounds coming from the animal he fully expected would one day be the most famous and celebrated show dog in the world . . . but who now lay before him as a wounded, fatally sick creature from whom he needed to protect his family.

His robe was still around Sam, and Hamish began shaking from cold. He dropped the rifle muzzle and put a palm to his eyes, drying the moisture, angry. Then he pulled a large piece of tamarack bark over to Sam and laid it across the two roots, making a sort of roof over the dog. He tucked the folds of material around him, being careful not to get near Sam's mouth, which he still believed carried a dangerous disease that had made the small dachshund go mad.

Hamish had instinctively grabbed his phone before running from the house. He pulled it from the pocket of the robe tucked around Sam and made a call.

"Sheriff. It's Hamish McCloud. Yes, I know what time it is. Just listen: call animal control and tell them that there's a dog that needs picking up on my property. He's sick, crazy—tried to harm one of my own, George. I winged him, but he's still alive. No . . . I can't finish it. You need to fetch him and . . . do whatever needs doing. He's

under the big fig tree next to my eastern gate. They can't
miss him. He's . . . uh, wrapped in my bathrobe. Yes, you
heard me."

Hamish closed the phone and looked down at the unmoving dog, breathing hard, looking back at him. He swung the rifle up toward the sky and fired it once, the blast echoing through the hills and making Sam flinch. "She'll need to hear that," Hamish said. "She'll need to know it's over and . . ." He trailed off.

He pulled his pajama collar high around his neck and leaned over Sam, looking into his eyes for the last time. He whispered, "You'll be warm, Sam." Hamish looked up into the sky and then back down, pain written on his face. "Thank you . . . for bringing me back to Heidy."

He turned and disappeared into the curtain of snow.

Sam rested, panting. He licked some snow, moistening his dry mouth, and then ate some ice. The robe's warmth was soothing and he closed his eyes, trying hard not to think more about this day of horror and madness. He was more tired than he'd ever been in his short life and was only dimly aware when other men arrived and he felt himself being lifted and carried through the trees. He was even less aware of being placed into a metal box in a truck and the door closing with darkness, once again, falling upon him.

SIXTEEN

- LASSIE -

Several hours later the light returned to Sam like drapes in a black room opening very slowly. After a few moments he remembered that his heart was broken.

Things were blurred. Shadowy. Wet.

Wet? thought Sam.

He was being kissed all over the face.

Licked.

Slowly, the face on the other end of the oddly rough

tongue doing the licking came into focus, inches from his. She was beautiful. A miniature greyhound, maybe—of exquisitely delicate features.

Slurp.

"Am I in heaven?" asked Sam.

"Certainly," cooed a voice like velvet. "And I'm Bambi's dead mother."

Sam picked up his head and looked around. Ancient bricks oozing water and slime curved over his head. Black, rusted bars stretched across in front of him. A round, dungeon-like space lay beyond, bathed in a familiar misty blue light. He could hear music and voices somewhere, echoing through watery tunnels. No, not heaven.

"Actually, my name is Madam. And you're still in Vermont. Fifty feet below it."

"Why are you licking my face?" said Sam.

"Because it's such a cute one. I'm also tidying it up."

Sam realized his head didn't throb with pain anymore. With a paw he felt that the bullet's gaping cut on his scalp had been sewn shut and the dried blood was gone. A needle and thread lay nearby on the filthy floor. Madam shrugged.

"I've . . . gotten quite good with that."

Sam rose unsteadily and walked toward the bars to look out. A crumbling spiral staircase descended from the darkness above. A single beam of pale moonlight found its way

down from some distant filthy window. In the middle of the round brick room sat a single old desk with piles of paper, a video player and a small TV on top: the source of the blue light that flickered across the bricks.

A sign on the desk said:

ADOPTION FORMS HERE.

Seven dogs sat piled on and around a single chair in the dark, watching the tiny screen. They turned their heads to look at Sam and said in chorus:

"Evenin'!"

Then they turned back to the old movie playing on the TV.

Sam noticed that his cage door was open. He moved out toward the desk. One of the dogs turned to Sam and said in a hushed, excited voice, "It's the last scene! Sooo, so great. Lassie was taken from her little boy and sold and sent away, then escaped and spent months lost and crossing the country struggling to get home and she's nearly dead and crawling to his school where the little boy has come out and spotted her . . ."

Sam looked at the screen. He watched the boy in the movie run to the filthy, wounded collie and embrace her. "Lassie, you've come home!" he said.

The mesmerized dogs erupted in a cascade of mournful howling and sobs, making Sam jump. They turned to each other and hugged happily. One gargantuan beast turned to Sam, wiped a tear and said, "*SUCH* a good flick!"

"How . . . many times have you all seen it?" asked Sam, wide-eyed.

The dogs looked at each other. One started counting on his paws.

"Well, lessee. . . . Every night for . . . for . . . how long, Blue?"

"Years," said the dog next to him. A blue pit bull. With lavender spots and chartreuse ears.

As an astonished Sam moved closer to them, he suddenly realized that they were the seven most ridiculous dogs he had ever seen. The seven most ridiculous *anything* he'd ever seen

"Meet the neighbors, pilgrim," said Madam, pointing to the biggest one, indistinguishable from a furry rhinoceros. "This is Tusk. His love of mailmen is a one-way affair."

A terrier mix the size of a yard mole stepped forward. "Wee Willy," said Madam. "Willy liked to lick noses. Alas, from the inside."

A nearly hairless mutt walked out with a face overwhelmed with wrinkles, piano wire hair and bulging eyeballs. "Here's Bug," said Madam. "An underappreciated beauty."

The blue pit bull mix stood up, the color of gummy bears. "Dear, sweet Ol' Blue. She clashed with her last owner's couch. She actually clashes with all couches.

"Fabio, stand up, please," urged Madam. Fabio—a lanky greyhound-pointer-beagle mix of some sort—did exactly that, standing on his two rear legs, which was good since he had no front legs whatsoever. "Fabio was born missing some things. But not a healthy self-image."

A bassett mix ambled out, tripping over jowls that draped like beach towels. "Here's Jeeves. Very important that he avoids breezes.

"And then finally, we have Pooft. Come out, dear."

A tiny black curly-haired mutt hopped forward. Sam stared. Seemed normal. "Wait," said Madam. Suddenly a three-foot flame rocketed out from his exhaust port accompanied by the sound of an old Chrysler backfiring. Pooft shot forward and hit the wall next to Sam. Behind, all the papers from the desk had blown off, leaving a few singed and smoking with a faint odor lingering in the air of, thankfully, French toast.

Pooft looked at Sam, somewhat embarrassed. "Bad kibble," he said.

Sam stared at the dogs, perplexed. "What breeds are you?"

The dogs glanced at each other, confused.

"We're dogs," said Madam.

"What *kind*?" said Sam.

Madam thought. "With skin," she said, satisfied.

Sam looked at them in horror. "Where am I?"

Then he knew. "Wait. I've heard about these places! It's the scary bedtime stories that dog parents tell their puppies about where they'll end up if they're not clean or groomed or . . . perfect."

Sam looked at the bars with disgust.

"This is a dog pound."

Madam moved in closer toward Sam. "No, no, no, handsome. It's not just any dog pound. It's the country's *worst*. It's where they send the hopeless cases. It's the end of the road. The unholiest of the unholy. The National Last-Ditch Dog Depository. And you . . . are the newest depositee."

Sam looked stunned. Then angry. "I'm no depositee. I'm an Austrian red dachshund."

The dogs looked back at him politely.

"I have a Duüglitz tuft!" said Sam.

Fabio stood on his only two legs, cleared his throat and struck a pose. "I have twelve nipples."

Sam looked around frantically. "I've gotta get back home. Which way is out?"

Madam pointed up the spiral stairs. Sam dashed up several and then stopped.

"The door's not locked," said Madam.

Sam looked surprised.

Madam smiled slightly. "They know we won't leave. We don't want to."

"Then what *do* you want?"

"Why, to be *taken*."

Sam frowned, then turned to go higher. He stopped again and looked down at Madam. "Come with me. You're not like those others. You're *perfect*."

Madam reached up with a paw, pushing off her fake, expertly sewn dog muzzle made of leather and snipped fur . . . revealing the snubbed flat nose of a cat.

"Nobody's perfect," she purred.

SEVENTEEN

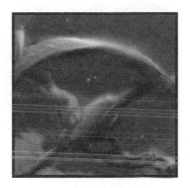

- BETRAYED -

Sam dashed out of the ancient fort and into the frigid night. He looked back to see a series of crumbling walls hewn from massive red granite. It looked like what it was: a forgotten prison from a long-ago war, rotting in a frozen marsh. A sign, leaning from the wind, read: **ADOPTIONS ON TUESDAYS, 1 P.M. TO 1:15 P.M.**

Someone had scratched out the times with a marker, scrawling underneath: DON'T BOTHER.

Where was he? The hills looked familiar. He was at the edge of a familiar city. He sniffed the freezing air. A thousand scents flooded in, but it wasn't difficult picking out the smoldering alder wood in the fireplace of Hamish's upstairs study. He sniffed. Home was about five miles away. Maybe four. He'd follow the river.

As Sam started off, he looked back at the gloomy stone citadel from which he'd just emerged. *Won't be coming back here,* he thought.

Back inside and below the old fort, down in its darkest recesses, the homeless, unwanted lost dogs of the National Last-Ditch Dog Depository pushed the start button on the VCR and huddled together as *Lassie Come Home* started again. Madam looked up the winding stairs that the strange new dachshund had just ascended. The others noticed her looking and looked at her. Then, on cue, they all said in a chorus: "He'll be back."

Staying to the shadows of the riverbank, Sam ran west. He would find Heidy and she would somehow understand that everything was a mistake—that it was Cassius, not he, that was the danger.

Breathing hard, Sam loped through the fresh snow, lit brightly by a newly emerged moon. His head throbbed as he reached a low draw in the hills where the wall crossed a stream, now frozen. A large drainpipe emerged below the stonework: the way he and Heidy would sneak out of the estate when she was supposed to be doing her chores. Sam stepped into its darkness. He froze at a familiar voice in the blackness inches from his face:

"They say poodles are the smartest breed. Alas, dear, departed Sam. *'Tis true.*"

Sam backed from the pipe, startled. Cassius emerged into the moonlight and stood over the dachshund, now balanced awkwardly in the rocks of the frozen stream. "Move aside," said Sam, regaining his composure.

"Poor, beautiful, perfect Sam the Lion. Your Heidy . . . she doesn't love you now, dear boy. You're . . . well, let's review." Cassius thought carefully, fluffing the curled fur around his ankles with his lips. ". . . Imperfect. Sick. Violent. *Ugly.*"

The words cut into Sam and found purchase in a mind still trying to make sense of the senseless. But he raised his head higher. "Move, Cassius. She still wants me."

"No. She has *me* now," said the poodle.

The words stung Sam as if they'd slapped him. The terrible truth behind the unspeakable events of the day came tumbling down upon Sam, and he grew dizzy. Everything had been a cruel hoax. Cassius was never after the baby. He was after *him*.

"Move away, Cassius," said Sam, desperation edging into his voice.

"You're not clear on this, dachshund. She doesn't want you now. You're not the perfect dog you were."

Sam looked at his reflection in the ice. A filthy, ripped face looked back, blood still caked to his fur.

"I will be again," said Sam. But Cassius was already stepping toward him, the perfectly combed balls of poodle fur blocking the moonlight and casting Sam into shadow. Sam stepped backward while Cassius lowered his head, stared intently and spoke low, each terrible word falling from his mouth with a rolling puff of steam into the frigid air:

"You know, dear Sam, some believe that for the dirty, unwanted, broken stray mongrels of the world . . . there is a guardian angel. I think that must be true. Those lesser dogs have nobody else, do they? Nobody but an angel would want them. They say she's quite beautiful . . . descending down a glimmering beam of blue light when death arrives . . . offering the flawed, unwanted souls a second chance. I think it's time you met her."

Cassius again stepped toward Sam, who again stepped

backward. "I'm not unwanted!" Sam said, his voice rising. "And I'm not *flawed*!"

Cassius smiled oddly and forced Sam backward another inch.

"Yes. You are."

At that precise moment, Sam's left rear foot stepped back onto the trigger plate of an open steel leg trap, freshly set for the winter beaver season. The jagged metal jaws came together several inches above Sam's foot, crushing the bone, the sound echoing off the Vermont hills like a rifle shot. Sam rolled onto his back, reflexively kicking the air, his mouth flying open in a tortured howl of pain swallowed up by the cruel silence of the falling snow in a day at long last exhausted of heartbreak.

EIGHTEEN

- ABYSS -

A cold dawn broke slow and heavy over McCloud Heavenly Acres. Downstairs, Uncle Hamish sat silently at the breakfast table, alone in his thoughts. Violett brought him coffee, which he took without speaking. He took the cup but held her hand and stared ahead blankly. Violett laid her other thin hand atop his unruly hair and gently smoothed it. Upstairs, Mrs. Beaglehole stood stiffly in the threshold of Heidy's bedroom door, peering in, as if waiting. In the large window seat before a dark sky, Heidy sat with knees curled to her chest, arms holding them tight. She stared out dully over the now white Vermont hills with spent eyes. There was simply no more moisture left in her body.

Cassius approached the girl silently. He sat and laid a long nose into the fold of her lap . . . and waited.

Heidy's hand released her other and dropped slowly down, as if thinking on its own. Her fingers alighted on the smooth brow of the poodle . . . and remained on his head.

Cassius closed his eyes and smiled.

As did Mrs. Beaglehole, still watching from the hall. She slowly closed the door.

Nobody in the McCloud house at that moment knew that only a quarter mile away, two men stood just outside the estate walls peering down at their beaver trap, trying to decide what sort of critter they had caught.

"Looks like a rat," said one.

"A blue ribbon big rat," said the other. "Three-legged rat now."

" 'Cept rats got naked tails. This one's furry."

When Sam let out a low whimper, the two trappers knew the creature was indeed something else. They pulled the halves of the trap apart and lifted the limp dog away. One wrapped a handkerchief around Sam's smashed leg

and secured it with a rubber band that had kept his matches attached to his box of cigarettes.

They carried Sam to their truck a mile away and placed him on the seat between them. In the warmth of the cab, the fog of Sam's mind slowly cleared, although the sights and sounds around him still seemed like a dream. And in that dream he watched through half-closed eyes as he was driven into town, where more men met the truck and huddled with the men who had found him. The second group of men handed over a small stack of money to the first and then carried Sam over to a different truck, the back of which was filled with small steel boxes. Sam's nose told him that they also contained dogs, unwanted and lost. He was placed inside a cage and the door closed and locked. Still too weak to stand, Sam peered through a crack in the steel door and watched the forested hills he'd explored with Heidy over recent months change to those far less familiar.

After many hours, the truck pulled up to a tall chain-link security fence that surrounded a vast array of very dark buildings with few windows. A sign next to the fence read:

NEW ENGLAND UNIVERSITY
RESEARCH LABS.

As the sun set, the skies again became leaden, and snow began to fall as the truck pulled into the complex. The dogs in the boxes around him sensed a change, and one by one, each began to utter low mournful howls. Through the door's crack, Sam watched as the gate closed behind him and the world beyond—the world of sunlight and dandelions and a girl's laughter and everything he'd known that was right and fair and good—receded into the distance. He knew with absolute certainty . . . like dogs know that a distant storm is approaching or that a stranger isn't to be trusted . . . he knew that world was gone forever.

NINETEEN

— 12:03:28 A.M. —

The following year, spring came early to the leafy hills surrounding University Research Labs before burning out in its usual fiery finale in fall.

It did the same the next year.

No, there will be no details recounted here to describe the indescribable events experienced by Sam and the other animals living beyond those terrible walls during this time. No good will come from dwelling on such horrors, and they are best left to the nightmares of feverish children and the dark imaginations of bullies who pull the wings off flies.

When the leaves returned in the third year, it was in the warming, rainy night air of April that our story and our dachshund return.

Three minutes, twenty-eight seconds after midnight, actually . . .

TWENTY

- ANGEL -

The gate guard for University Research Labs looked up from what he was reading and peered through the window of his little booth to see thousands of white rats running toward him.

This normally would have been enough to wrest his attention from a comic book, but it was the two hundred dogs behind them that brought him to his feet spewing forth a half-chewed Butterfinger from his mouth.

He jumped outside his booth into the drizzle to better see what appeared to be a biblical plague descending on his little spot on the planet. Like a swarm of ants, the rats and dogs funneled down from the dark lab buildings, from which now blared forth an emergency siren announcing the obvious.

It was a breakout.

The guard squinted and refused to believe what he thought he saw at the front of the phalanx of hopping, running, stumbling animals: Two beagles ran side by side, strapped across their backs a sort of missile launcher made of a half-curved aluminum rain gutter. Within this lay the now three-legged Sam, aimed and ready to launch like a furry bullet in a hot dog bun. Stretched onto the dachshund's nose was a human's latex glove, its index finger filled with several ounces of Elmer's glue hardened rock solid. The guard believed it was aimed directly at his nose.

This image alone was enough for the guard to abandon all romantic notions of a Custer-like last stand, and he threw himself backward toward the chain-link gate behind him, scrambling upward and away from what he believed to be certain death.

At precisely nine feet from the guard booth, the two beagles threw out their front paws and came to an abrupt stop, sending Sam shooting out the half-pipe and up. He sailed straight and true through the night air, feet back, tail

straight, hitting the electric gate's recessed green Open button with the index finger of the glove on his nose. He clung to the electric junction box with his three feet like a huge squirrel while the massive gate began to roll aside, opening a space to escape for the approaching horde of animals.

"FORWARD! GO! C'MON! FASTER!" yelled Sam to the rats and dogs, now streaming through the ever-enlarging space and toward the street—and freedom—below the facility. Sam looked back to the lab buildings and saw that people began to emerge on the heels of the last dogs. *"GO GO GO DON'T LOOK BEHIND!"*

Another beagle struggled in the back, hampered by bandages that circled his middle covering the burns given him to test a new antiseptic ointment. The men behind were almost on him. The dog yelled at Sam: *"Go on without me! (puff puff puff) I'm not gonna make it!"*

"Yes, you are! Don't stop!" said Sam. He pressed the red Close button on the gate with his latex nose finger. The gate began rolling shut again, all the animals safely through . . . except for the struggling beagle, closing fast, the lab people reaching out for him only two yards behind.

With a metallic bang, the gate slammed shut, the beagle having slid through with only a few hairs at the end of his tail getting severed by the metal portal. Unable to stop in time, the men piled into the chain link in a tangle of limbs and squashed bodies.

Sam had freed the others but remained inside the perimeter. He leapt to the roof of the guardhouse, inches from the fingers of several lab workers. Even now, with only three legs, his former gymnastic instincts returned to carry him as he leapt from the roof to the light pole to the gate, up the chain link and through the razor wire coiled across its top, several of the sharp daggers tearing the flesh across his back as he went.

Sam dropped to the wet pavement with a howl of pain, spraining his remaining rear leg. Shaking off the latex glove from his nose, he looked to the other side of the street, where the last of the beagles were scrambling to the uncertain destiny of a life far away from people. Then he looked back to the workers in the white coats still piled in a tangle on the other side of the gate, breathing hard, staring at him from three feet away. Sam's sprained leg was near useless, and he couldn't run at all now. They had only to open the gate to reach him and return him to the horrors he'd just left.

A woman he recognized . . . the only human in that place who had ever looked at him with something besides cold disinterest . . . the one who had risked a rare, gentle stroke of her fingers across his shaking head at his darkest moments of pain and fear . . . she stood at the gate's switch box, hand poised over the green Open button.

"Push it! Push it, Simmons!" screamed one of the men. "Push it or you're fired!"

Sam looked at the woman, who smiled back with a look something between pain and relief and shame. She dropped her hand to her side.

"SIMMONS!" the man yelled, not believing what he was watching.

Sam turned and hobbled down the highway into the darkness, knowing that the gate would open soon regardless. Cars roared past him, their lights stabbing through the mist like searchlights, confusing him. The sirens at the lab grew distant, but he didn't dare stop, now nearly dragging the rear of his long torso along the slippery pavement. He saw the lights of a service station across the highway, and the prospect of a hiding place lured him to cross the expanse of road.

He had nearly crossed the final lane when the pickup truck swerved and braked after its lights found the small dog directly in front of it. The tire hit Sam on his upper hip, sending him spinning onto the shoulder of the road.

Sam lay there, spent and breathing hard. Pain racked his tiny body, moving in torturous waves that ebbed and flowed from sources too numerous to count. He lay on his back and stared up at the sky, cold, cruel and black. He licked the air for rain, desperate to slake a parched and raw throat. His mind whirled from exhaustion and pain, and his thoughts became muddy, confused.

The sky suddenly grew lighter, and the falling mist sparkled like tiny diamonds. Sam opened his eyes wider. Suddenly he was doused in the brilliance of a blinding white light that seemed to descend on his broken body.

"Push the button, Simmons!" screamed one of the men.
"Push it or you're fired!"

Despite the mental fog, his mind traveled back to what Cassius had said that terrible night over three years ago: that for the lost and unwanted dogs of the world, a guardian angel comes calling at their final moments.

This, the dazzling brilliance suddenly flooding his

senses and surrounding his world . . . this surely must be *that*.

He could feel his brutalized body lifting . . . floating up from the freezing road.

Sam closed his eyes and waited.

TWENTY-ONE

– LIFTED –

The tall young man stood in the rain staring down at the small panting dog lying on the wet road. He ran his flashlight across the tiny body and was surprised to see the foot missing. For a moment he thought it might have been the result of the impact, but he quickly saw that the stump was long healed. Sam's short breaths told the man that a broken rib lay below his shaking chest. He saw the shallow rips that covered the dog's flesh and wondered how they had happened.

Reaching down, he slipped rough, callused hands below the limp form and lifted him from the pavement. He carried the wounded dog to his truck and laid him on his dirty coat, coiled on the passenger floor.

The man pulled back onto the highway and drove off into the rainy night, pointed to somewhere else far, far from heaven.

TWENTY-TWO

- JAM -

"Leggle."

Sam heard this word and some chuckling as he finally woke fully a few days later. He winced in pain, but it wasn't the searing pain on the street from before. He looked down at his body, which was almost completely swaddled in bandages. He looked up to see a man fiddling with the lengths of twine, holding on to something that one doesn't normally see attached to dogs:

A ladle. Small, made of steel, for scooping gravy.

Loops of twine affixed the ladle to the stump of his long-missing leg.

"A leggle," the man said to himself, amused. He stopped chuckling when he saw that Sam's eyes were open. "Well, little buddy. Back to the land of the livin', I see. I was worried. Good." He stood up and looked down at the broken dachshund curled in the towel on his worn couch. "I gotta go to work. You just stay put, hang loose, heal up. I'll be back at five." He put on a torn coat and looked around the tiny apartment, dingy but neat. He pointed to the sink. "Wouldn't be bad if you did a few dishes."

At the door he turned around. "Leggle!" he said, chuckling again. "I'll bring home some food. Any requests?"

Soup, thought Sam, looking at his new leg. *I'll serve.*

The man stared at Sam with a sad smile. "Life. She don't much like either of us, does she?" He closed the door.

Sam lifted his leggle and waved it around a bit. Might work. He put his head back down and closed his eyes. He would think about what to do later, after his wounds and rib healed, when his strength returned. He fell asleep, smiling faintly. *I'll serve the soup.* It was a good joke.

He hadn't thought of anything funny for almost three years.

For the next few months, Sam's life followed the routine of the Rough-Handed Man's, wavering little. Each morning they would leave after a breakfast of scrambled eggs and sausage, Sam's steel leggle clattering as they both descended the steps of the tiny apartment behind the auto repair shop. With the help of his new foot, Sam would leap into the cab of the beaten pickup truck and ride to the man's work at a construction site. Sam put his back feet on the seat and propped his front two on the dashboard to better observe the world up ahead, being careful not to think about anything and *anyone* from the distant world behind him. Because behind him was where it was going to stay, and if he thought about it much, a darkness would descend that he might not ever escape from.

Every day, the man would park under a tree, roll down the windows, leave a bowl of water on the cab floor and give Sam a pat on the head before walking to the huge building that was under construction. At lunch, the man returned and they often ate peanut butter sandwiches together. Peanut butter, Sam decided, was not his new favorite food, as his tongue would usually get stuck to the roof of his long mouth and the Rough-Handed Man would have to pry it off with a wooden coffee stirrer. At 5 P.M. the man would return and they would go home and watch TV and often have—to Sam's relief--french fries. At bedtime, the man would reach to pet Sam on his head, and Sam would pull away slightly for reasons neither understood but both came to accept.

And that was about it. Until one Friday.

It was dark and almost ten o'clock, and the man hadn't returned to the truck. Sam stood up and peered over the door into the work site. A few cars remained, and there was a light inside. People were still in there doing something, but Sam couldn't imagine what it was. Maybe a game of some sort. He could hear voices. An occasional whoop or cheer. Or groan.

Suddenly Sam saw the man running full speed out from the building, keys in hand. Several large men followed, chasing. Sam could hear the man screaming the same thing repeatedly: "I'LL PAY IT BACK! I'LL PAY IT BACK!" He dove into the cab of the truck, but one of his pursuers grabbed the door, keeping him from closing it. As the man frantically pulled, the other man tried to reach around the door to grab his neck. The Rough-Handed Man turned to Sam and screamed, "DON'T LET 'EM IN! DON'T LET 'EM IN!"

Sam had no idea what was going on, but it seemed clear enough that life would be generally better without the other men getting into the truck, so he curled his lips halfway up to his skull and let loose a display of saliva-spewing, teeth-snapping dog fury of such fierce proportions, the sight of it stopped the approaching men like a wall of skunk stink.

Even the Rough-Handed Man, still struggling with the door, couldn't help but be shocked, and he let out a low "Wow" in admiration of the performance.

The man got the door closed and, with the help of Sam's rabid Tasmanian devil imitation, sped the truck away with squealing tires, leaving the very angry men behind screaming unfamiliar words.

The Rough-Handed Man looked worried as he sped away and turned around to see if they were being followed.

They weren't. His pursuers receded from view, their shouts getting lost finally in the wind noise. The man looked at Sam sitting on the seat next to him, looking peaceful, and started to laugh . . . and then began singing an old sailors' song: *"Farewell and adieu to you, fair Spanish ladies . . ."*

Sam thought this was hilarious and joined in, his muzzle pointed high with matching howls.

But after a while, the man looked ahead and thought very, very hard about the mess he was in. Sam had never seen such fear on a human being's face before.

That night they ate in silence while the man paced the small rooms, deep in disturbed thought. Then he placed Sam on a chair and sat opposite him. He clasped his hands, leaned close and spoke to Sam in the way that people speak at length to dogs when they're frightened or excited or have been alone for too long and gone slightly crazy.

"Hey, ol' buddy. We've . . . You haven't done too bad by me, have ya?"

"I have a big spoon for a foot. Could be worse," said Sam.

"I . . . I'm in a bit of a jam. There's some people I owe a lot of . . . stuff. I don't have it. But there's a way—a small chance, really—that I could get it. You could have somethin' to do with it."

"Me?" said Sam.

"I'm askin' a lot. Maybe everything."

"You want my half of the french fries."

The man's face was twisted in the worst sort of painful grimace Sam had ever seen. He reached to pat Sam's head but then pulled his hand back, almost embarrassed.

"What I'm asking, little buddy," he said, "is for you to forgive me."

Sam had no idea why he said that.

By the next terrible night . . . the night where this book began, he would.

TWENTY-THREE

- LEAVE -

As the Rough-Handed Man carried Sam down into the dark depths of the building at the edge of the city, the sights and smells of human beings and money and cruelty couldn't overwhelm an even larger sense that the three-legged dog was feeling:

Fear.

His own . . . and surprisingly, the man's. It radiated up from his huge hands, cradling Sam's bottom and chest as they moved toward the dog-fighting pit below the brilliant light. But there was something else Sam smelled besides the man's sweat and fear:

Shame.

Sam sensed and saw it on the man's face as he gently lowered Sam into the tiny arena, now surrounded by yelling faces and waving money. *Shame.* The man's eyes avoided Sam, and he turned to make some sort of arrangement with all the money-waving men.

Sam realized now that it was that, the money, that this was all about. And the trembling spitting screaming beast that ached to get at Sam across the pit was the obstacle for the man getting it.

Sam was meant to fight. And win. And survive.

Not likely.

Which is why Sam lay down against the wall and closed his eyes, allowing—for the first time in many years—the memories of a long-past life to flood his mind before the coming violence descended upon his tiny body. He was back in the grass of Vermont, running, a girl's voice calling his name . . . when another familiar voice broke through.

"BUDDY!"

Sam opened his eyes and looked up at the crowd of faces. He saw the Rough-Handed Man looking down at him.

But he saw something just below him. A ragged poster

next to others lining the filthy walls of the pit. It was for the Westminster Dog Show in New York City. It was the large picture of a dog at the center of it that made Sam sit up and squint into the glare of overhead lights.

It was a huge poodle. Looking gorgeous and regal and very, very familiar.

Cassius.

A word that he had long blocked out along with the rest of his memories. A word that suddenly fell on his mind like a butcher's cleaver.

"Cassius!" said Sam loudly. *"CASSIUS!"*

The crowd heard a bark from the absurd, tiny dog lying in the pit waiting for death.

Silence.

Two hundred voices suddenly went still, their waving hands grasping the money stopped. The Rough-Handed Man stared, as did the others, waiting. Even the great snarling pit bull opposite Sam froze.

Cassius. The destroyer of worlds . . . Sam's world.

Cassius was alive!

If only it were *he* that stood five feet away at this moment, thought Sam, rather than the mindless, broken pit bull that was.

That would be something to live for. To die for.

To kill for.

Cassius is still out there.

That single thought . . . the seed of an unfinished idea . . . was enough to hook the frayed remnant that had become Sam's life and keep him from sinking.

The stunned crowd watched in disbelief as Sam got to his feet. His eyes, now wide and focused, scanned the small pit and wood wall that surrounded it . . . and the killing machine opposite his nose.

Gotta get out of this place! he thought, his mind racing, roaring, cooking at full boil.

But first he had to deal with the huge saliva-dripping problem in front of him. He dug deep for the instincts and skills from a distant time in his life.

Time to change the rules.

"Let him go!" Sam barked to the man holding back the pit bull. *"NOW!"*

The pit bull opposite was released, but before the great dog could lunge, Sam was rushing *him*. The massive jaws snapped at Sam's tiny head but found only air, for Sam had dropped low and slid between his wide-set legs as if on ice, emerging below the dog's tail. Spinning, Sam leapt atop the beast's back and careened off his head like a squirrel bouncing across a rock in a stream. But as Sam passed the smooth head, his stainless steel leggle whacked the surprised beast on the skull, stunning him, making him wobble on his spread feet.

Sam raced around the perimeter at blinding speed, the bigger dog spinning dizzyingly in the opposite direction,

vainly trying to intercept the smaller, faster one . . . all of which made Sam look like the tiny ball spinning around a giant roulette wheel.

The crowd screamed. *This* they'd never seen before. The Rough-Handed Man simply sat, mouth slightly open, eyes wide in shock.

The pit bull was powerful but slower than the tiny target, and Sam stayed in front of his flashing teeth. Over and over, Sam would leap high on the wall and fall atop the big dog's head with a well-aimed whack of the steel ladle. But this would not be enough. It only drove the pit bull into further rage, the snot blowing from his flared black nostrils like dragon's breath. It set itself up for one final run straight at Sam, backed up against the wall.

The big dog kept his head low, knowing Sam's favorite trick. The muscled legs propelled the fighting machine forward with shocking power, and his head was nearly upon Sam when the dachshund leapt straight up, four feet like a sprung mattress spring. He wrapped his front legs around the surprised fist of the Rough-Handed Man leaning over the railing . . . and hung on.

The pit bull never saw Sam do this and to this day remembers none of it, for when he hit the wall with the top of his pointed head, he was knocked clean into blissful unconsciousness, where he immediately commenced a dream of being stuck inside a locked closet filled with expensive shoes and beef liver and then eating his way out: the default fantasy for all pit bulls.

The crowd sat stunned, silent. They turned their eyes up to Sam, still dangling on the Rough-Handed Man's arm, who lifted the victorious dachshund and placed him on the wall before him. Slowly and silently, men began handing fistfuls of cash to the man, laying them in little piles next to his dog. Their bets.

It was a lot of money.

Sam looked up at the only small window above the crowd's heads, the full moon shining brilliantly beyond the distant horizon. He looked back over at the man's eyes and looked at him squarely. Even if this human being would have understood the dog, no words were needed:

It was time for Sam to leave.

The Rough-Handed Man looked back into the eyes of the dog that he'd nursed back from the edge of death many months ago, and he smiled.

Then with a wink he stared squarely at Sam and began singing under his breath: *"Farewell and adieu to you, fair Spanish ladies . . ."*

Instantly, Sam hopped atop the man's head and then leapt to another two feet behind him. That man threw his hands up to try to catch the bounding dog, but Sam was long gone to the next noggin. And the next, moving ever closer to the window behind them all as the men went wild again and roared, pushing closer and reaching to stop the head-leaping runaway.

Dogs just don't escape, they were all thinking. Not *here*!

And especially not one that took their money.

Food and drink cups and bottles hurtled toward Sam,

but the dog simply ducked and dodged the missiles. Two men spotted his destination and moved to block the tiny window. Now where? Grimy hands reached for him, tearing at the folds of his skin but finding no purchase with the smooth coat of fur. Sam moved in jerky, frantic changes of directions as he looked for any escape, any exit, any possible path to freedom, but the enraged crowd only closed in tighter. The lights went out and the room fell into darkness.

Suddenly a different voice—a dog's voice—cut through the roar, as if someone had turned the crowd's volume control down: *"'Ere, lad! Over 'ere!"*

"Hey! What? Who was that?"

He heard it again.

"Over 'ere, doggy doggy!"

Sam couldn't see the caller, but he leapt across more heads toward the voice, trusting its urgency. There was no other option.

"The tunnel! Go for the bloody tunnel!" said the stranger with a metallic echo. *"Follow me melodious voice!"*

Sam spied a small opening at the base of the filthy wall at the back of the room—a heating duct from where the voice emerged. Sam went for it. He shot into the dark hole, but a large red-faced man with a stinking, fuming cigar clenched in angry teeth grabbed the weakest link in any dog chase: Sam's tail.

Sam came to a sudden stop in the duct. Then he was

dragged backward toward the man's huge, red bald head, which was now wholly inserted into the aluminum tunnel. Sam had little choice but to push the nuclear button in a dog's world of survival:

He peed.

This, among other more useful results, extinguished the cigar.

TWENTY-FOUR

– CURTAINS –

Sam wiggled through the heating vent duct like a rat in a drainpipe, the sounds of the hollering men growing distant behind him. He saw a light ahead and aimed for it. He hit a wall grate and tumbled out into a filthy stairwell. The source of the voice stood staring at him nervously on the steps.

It was—from Sam's best guess—a Scottish terrier–hyena–dust mop mix.

One that appeared to have been plugged into an electrical socket while standing in a dish of muddy water.

"Who are you?" said Sam.

"No! 'Oo are YOU?" said the beast with an odd Scottish lilt.

"You called for me to run into the duct!"

"No, I called for one o' them sixty-pound murder 'n' mayhem machines. And out pops a peewee tofu pup wearin' a kitchen spoon. Now what bloody good are you?"

"What good am I *for what*?" said Sam.

He followed the mutt's nervous glance down the stairs.

A dozen serious, murderous-looking feral cats crept up from the building's depths straight toward them.

The new dog looked at Sam and shrugged.

"It 'appens that in regards to the house management, I am a little behind on me mouse payments."

He pointed at his pursuers.

"Sic 'em, killer."

Suddenly a metal door flew open on the landing just behind the gang of cats, out of which tumbled a gaggle of men. The large bald one—still with a soggy cigar in his mouth—was wiping his head dry of defensive dachshund pee. The damp man yelled, "THERE! THERE! GET HIM!"

Sam spun and dashed up the stairs, the other dog following. Sam hit the roof door and found himself on an empty flat rooftop four stories above the streets in the driving rain of a summer night's thunderstorm. The skies lit up and cracked in rolling rumbles.

The gang of cats emerged from the doorway, fifty feet opposite them. They fanned out to attack, crouching low.

The men followed. Pulling their shirts over their heads against the rain, they too fanned out. Sam and the mutt's backs were now up against a low wall at the corner of the roof sixty feet above the concrete.

Trapped.

The men and cats started moving in on them.

"Well, now," said the new dog without taking his eyes off their assailants. "Guess yer pretty glad I got ya out o' that bit o' trouble down there, Sammy lad."

Sam glared at the dog. "How did you know my name was Sam?"

"Well, now. It's not Maurice Tenderboogers, is it?"

"No."

"Bubbles Graboff?"

"No."

"Peaches?"

"No."

"Good, 'cause that's my name. That leaves Sam."

Sam ignored this curious logic because the men were getting closer and they were holding wooden clubs and slapping them on their sweaty hands. Within moments they and the rabid pack of cats would be upon the filthy, disheveled, mud- and sweat-caked little pair.

"Looks like it's curtains for us, Sammy," whispered Peaches, staring at their approaching attackers. "You and me, we've been through a lot together. Experienced all the ups and downs o' life. I'd like t' just say that if you and I 'ave to depart this cruel world . . ." He licked his paw and smoothed the clot of lawn sod on his head. ". . . we'll be goin' out lookin' our very best."

Sam twitched.

Going out lookin' our best . . . repeated Sam to himself.

And then in the span of a single second . . . in the same

tiny amount of time it takes for the most complex adventure to spool out in a dream—it all just popped into Sam's mind:

How to get to Cassius.

Born instantly in all its devious complexity—whole and complete:

Going out lookin' our best.

Sam's face lit up, in a dark sort of way.

Sam looked around. He spotted what he was looking for. Jumping onto the low wall, he swung the steel ladle on his stump up and hooked it onto a telephone cable stretching down to a junction box at the street four floors down. Hanging upside down by his chrome foot in the driving rain and holding on to the wall, he was about to let go when he looked back at Peaches.

"You want to come or do you have other plans?"

The strange dog turned around to see what looked like the army from hell coming for them. He turned back to Sam.

"Depends. Where we going?"

"To destroy the International Westminster Dog Show in front of the world."

Peaches blinked.

"Or we could just hide in a Dumpster," said the mutt.

The men and feral cats were running at them now, hands and claws stretched out.

"Alas," said Peaches, staring at the looming mob. "No time."

Suddenly a white figure dashed in front of them from the left, skidding to a halt between the dogs and their pursuers. The huge pit bull killing machine Sam had just vanquished moments before stood there, legs apart, head low, teeth flashing and drool pooling on the pavement below his curled lips.

But he faced the men and cats, who wisely started backing up.

Turning his great square, bruised head back toward Sam, he said "GO!" Then he grinned and added, "Before I tried to kill you, you asked if there was anything I'd rather be doing. It came to me: Musical theater! Go!"

Sam saluted the bull terrier, turned and leapt for the telephone cable. He hooked the soup ladle on the wire and hung upside down. He looked back at Peaches and said, "Plane's leaving!" Peaches leapt onto Sam's upside-down back and sank claws into Sam's belly, making him wince. Sam let go of the wall and the three-legged dachshund and frazzled, doggy dust mop slid down the rain-soaked cable below a silver soup spoon, down into the driving storm, down toward the flooded street that led away from town and away from trouble and directly toward far, far more.

TWENTY-FIVE

- RETURN -

In the basement of the old stone fort on the edge of town, the eight depositees of the National Last-Ditch Dog Depository were awakened by a sound different from the muffled sounds of the summer storm they'd heard all night.

As always for the last many years, they'd slept in a pile, so untangling was a bit of a chore. Pooft yawned, politely minding where his inflammatory opposite end was pointed.

Wee Willy pulled himself out from between Tusk's toes, where it was always warm. Ol' Blue stretched a lavender leg. Bug rubbed his eyes with a paw, being careful not to knock one out. Fabio hopped onto his remaining two feet, stretching like a ballerina. And Madam adjusted her self-sewn Great Dane muzzle as she climbed out from below the blanket that was Jeeves's left jowl.

They all heard the same thing coming from outside the bars of their cage. The television. A little boy's voice:

"Lassie, you've come home!"

The dogs stumbled out of their enclosure past the always-unlocked cage door and blinked into the darkness. As thunder rolled somewhere above and lightning flashed, the dark room exploded into brilliance. Madam coolly stared at a vaguely familiar spoon-legged dachshund sitting atop the desk in the middle of the dungeon-like brick room.

"Handsome," purred Madam, "is back."

The little TV was on and playing their only movie: the little boy on the screen hugged his achingly beautiful pet.

Sam turned down the volume with his mouth. He glanced at Peaches, watching from the shadows, and then faced the others. He pointed to the screen and spoke with a different, harder voice than he had years before.

" 'Lassie, you've come home!' the boy says. He cries. He holds her. He hugs her. And he tells her again . . ."

Sam leaned in close to the dogs.

" ' . . . You've . . . come . . . home.' "

Sam pushed the power knob and the picture went black.

"WE," Sam roared, "WILL NEVER HEAR THAT!"

The dogs jumped. Peaches ducked. Sam began to pace across the top of the table, throwing glances at his audience.

"They aren't coming, you know," said Sam. "The families in their big boxy cars and the kids piling out to come down here to this wretched hole, put their faces to the bars, point at your crooked, runny noses and say, 'THAT one, Mommy. That's the one we'll take home and give a wicker bed and an old pillow to sleep on, the one we'll give a lap to rest his head on while we read a book . . . the one who'll curl up with us when we're sick or sad or just in need of someone to *LOVE*.' "

Sam spat out that final word as if it was something disgusting.

The dogs looked at Sam with a look that was new for them. Something between shock and sorrow and a deep and mournful pain that comes from finally seeing something unthinkably awful that you'd struggled to ignore.

Sam continued. "They are not coming for you. Ever. Because they have been fooled. And seduced. And stolen from you by *the others*." Sam dropped a rolled-up poster to the floor, where it unspooled. The dogs read it:

THE **Westminster Championship Dog Show**
COMING TO NEW YORK IN THREE DAYS

They all gasped at the magnificent dogs illustrating the words . . . their noses and legs and ears and fur all breathtakingly *perfect*.

"Lassie, you've come home!" said the
voice of a boy on the screen.

They'd never seen such animals.

Wee Willy walked up closer to the poster and whistled a low whistle of awe. He was looking at a picture of Cassius, standing largest in the center.

"Zowie. *That's* a dog."

"Yes," said Sam, cool, hiding his real emotions. "He is. And he . . . and all the rest of them . . . is why you will wait here forever while they take what should be yours. *Because you're flawed and they're not.*"

Sam snapped the movie on again. The boy was running toward the English horizon with Lassie at his heels, her shiny coat of fur flowing like threaded gold in a stream.

There then arose a sound new to the dark and terrible walls of the National Last-Ditch Dog Depository: a howling of a fresh and terrifying pitch . . . a cry not for food but of pride and vengeance.

Sam pointed to the Westminster poster. "In three days, they're coming to their grand palace of perfection. They and their human beings who don't want you. Who don't need you . . ."

Sam moved closer to the dogs.

". . . but I do."

Peaches looked at the dogs' faces. They were lit, glowing, alive. Sam's voice rose higher.

"Help me! Help me go to their great house of self-worship in New York City . . . and before the whole world

153

watching on their TVs, do to *them* what they've done to *you* . . ."

The dogs sat rigid, waiting.

". . . WRECK 'EM! WRECK *WESTMINSTER!*"

"WRECK WESTMINSTER!" they all chorused, leaping and bouncing. Even Madam showed explosive emotion, which for a cat means the subtle flaring of nostrils while looking bored.

Pooft backed up to the Westminster poster and shot a burst of flame from his afterburner, reducing it to glowing embers. He rocketed across the room in the opposite direction and hit a pail of dog food, exploding it like brown confetti.

From atop the desk, Sam and Peaches watched this gaggle of unwanted outcasts celebrate their new mission in life . . . pointing their noses high and howling to a moon they hadn't seen in years . . . but soon would.

TWENTY-SIX

– FLYER –

If Mr. Flemmie Croup, the sole administrator, caretaker and poop scooper of the National Dog Depository for the past forty-six years, had been just five minutes earlier in waking up the next morning . . . if he had been just one mile per hour faster in walking to work . . . if he had been only slightly less patient with feeding the squirrels in the freight yard that morning and had chucked the whole stale baguette at them instead of breaking it up into pieces . . .

then he might have actually stumbled into the dog escapees dashing out the front door ten minutes before dawn and he would have stopped the grand enterprise cold right there, leaving this book without an ending.

But he was not.

And he did not.

And it has one.

Mr. Croup arrived as always at three minutes *after* dawn and found the front door wide open and the dreadful building wholly absent of its seven permanent occupants. After wandering around tidying up, he then did what he'd never done in those forty-six years: He took the day off. And he went home for a bubble bath, in which he pondered in bubbly relish the thought that whatever sort of day his former depositees were about to experience . . . whatever trouble, mischief or harrowing mayhem they were to wander into . . . it would, without doubt, be the best day of their miserable lonely lives.

He was right.

The dawn broke in a sky clearing of the previous night's storm clouds. The Manhattan Flyer sped southward toward New York City with nine freeloading passengers atop its streamlined engine. They'd dropped from a trestle stretching over the rails back in Vermont after the engineer had slowed on spying what appeared to be a cowboy wearing a tutu sitting on the tracks reading a newspaper. On inspection, the trainman found it to be an old smashed store mannequin propped up with sticks, dressed in folds of pink wall insulation and a discarded straw hat. He continued southward, but now with a commando squad of unwanted mutts sitting directly above his head.

Soon, the steel pinnacles of New York City appeared on the brightening horizon. Most of the dogs were rehearsing the elaborate plan that Sam had explained to them the night before. But they also stole excited glances at a world speeding by them that they'd simply never really known existed.

Freshly woken, Sam lay on his back next to the roaring diesel exhaust, absorbing the warmth, looking at the clearing sky, thinking about what he had to do.

Peaches stared down at him.

"Sammy. I heard ya sneezin' durin' your nappy. But it weren't sneezes you was blurtin' out but a name: Cassius. Cassius. Cassius."

Sam shrugged.

"This Cassius chap . . . 'Ee's up ahead somewhere, ain't he? 'Ee's what this 'ole thing is about, I'm thinkin'."

Sam didn't say anything.

"It won't be a kiss you'll be givin' yer Cassius, will it?"

Silence.

"Oh, lad, it's a bad thing ya got in mind. I wouldn't be sayin' this if we wasn't such lifelong mates. I think yer using those poor blokes." Peaches looked at the other dogs farther back on the engine, pointing out the sights speeding by.

"They had nothing. Now they have a purpose," said Sam, stretching.

"Aye. Purpose 'n' pooches," sighed the odd dog. "Not much to that. They're not designed to catch a mouse. They're not meant to bring down a gallopin' wildebleedin' beast. Don't round up cows or sheep or pick up a log with their nose." He spat. "There is only one thing we silly slobbering furbags are put on this earth to do."

Peaches moved in close to Sam and pointed to the lights of Manhattan ahead. "This ain't it, lad."

Sam looked at him and said nothing. He turned and moved to the front edge of the roaring engine and raised himself on his rear legs—both bone and steel, his body upright like a sail, leaning forward, ears flowing backward into the morning's rising sun. The dachshund closed his eyes, his front paws pushed wide with the rushing wind, as if to embrace the sparkling city that sped closer . . . and a destiny darker than the other dogs suspected.

"Storm's over," Sam said.

"Not yet," said the little mutt quietly.

TWENTY-SEVEN

— QUACK —

Midnight.

New York City.

Two days before the big dog show.

Eldon P. Liddle, night watchman for Madison Square Garden, was dozing on the arena's roof in a lawn chair, as he always did on balmy summer New York nights. But it was quite breezy, and the sound of the wind through the decorative palm trees lining the roof's round edge woke Eldon just in time for him to see Jeeves come into view.

Eldon noted that Jeeves wasn't a particularly beautiful dog. Not like the ones that came every year and were due the next morning to prance around the arena far below him. This dog's jowls, for instance, were extraordinarily enormous and inflated like a flapping beach towel in the wind, floating the animal twelve feet from Eldon's stupefied face and 200 feet above the ground. A string wrapped around Jeeves's chest disappeared down toward the street, presumably, thought Eldon, to a gang of dog-flying terrorists in the parking lot.

Startled into petrified inaction, Eldon watched Jeeves drift on the breeze like a slobbering kite, scanning the items on the roof with the help of sharp eyes and a full moon. Jeeves noted three things as he floated: A huge water tank on stilts, several palm trees in large wooden dirt planters, and a very large roof skylight over the center of the arena below.

Jeeves motioned to be pulled back down. As the hound dog descended, Jeeves happened to look over at security guard Eldon P. Liddle and—giddy with the excitement of a newly purposeful life—did something that would cause the poor man to quit at the end of his shift:

He flapped his wings and quacked.

161

TWENTY-EIGHT

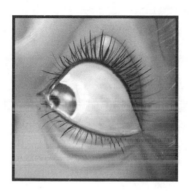

- BORROWING -

Noon.

One day before the big show.

Mrs. Corinthian Nutbush—last seen three years before, strapped to a Vermont ambulance gurney without most of her clothes—walked out the front doors having freshly registered her new long-haired dachshund, Mr. Toodles, for the Westminster competition. As usual, Mrs. Nutbush was wrapped from head to foot in the fur of many of the world's rarest animals. On this day, it was leopard, chinchilla, baby seal, and the rare Peruvian long-haired blue vole, the latter species having only a dozen known individuals left on the planet before Mrs. Nutbush's hat was made from ten of them.

Her Mr. Toodles led the way on a jeweled leash.

After tucking her priceless Westminster credentials inside her purse, Mrs. Nutbush moved into Central Park and paused to sit on a bench in front of the east fountain, as the stress of preparing for the world's most important dog show was wearing on a giant gopher-like woman her age.

She dozed off while Mr. Toodles licked up the pigeon droppings, whose taste he found similar to Junior Mints.

Mr. Toodles looked up from his brunch to see what at first he thought was a spotted mouse with the end of a long string in its mouth emerge from the hedge, run up Mrs. Nutbush's seal boot and disappear below her coat. Mr. Toodles sat down and continued tracking the creature by the small movements he could see it make as it traversed the towering peaks and valleys amidst the generous acreage below Mrs. Nutbush's clothes. The dachshund watched, fascinated, as the rodent scampered through the coat, the handbag, both her gloves, the loops on the back of the boots, and then finally up to her scarf around the mighty Nutbush neck.

It wasn't until Mr. Toodles saw the little creature actually drop the string temporarily, creep up the snoring woman's face and poke its head deep into the vastness of her right nostril that he finally realized that the creature wasn't a mouse at all but a three-ounce dog. He knew this because when the tiny mutt pulled his head out from the Nutbush honker, he turned around, looked down at the staring dachshund and said, *"If you yodel, there's an echo!"*

This is also when Mrs. Nutbush awoke to find what she believed to be a baby rat on her upper lip. She screamed and leapt to her feet as though stuck by an electric cattle prod while Wee Willy grabbed the string again and made a swan dive into the bottomless mine shaft of her cleavage. This sent the president of the Vermont Dachshund Club into a windmilling frenzy of self body-slapping and high kicks. As Wee Willy's movements below the clothing grew even more athletic, Mrs. Nutbush began to tear her clothes completely off.

This was the plan.

Mr. Toodles sat motionless on the sidewalk, chewing his snacks and watching with keen interest as his female human—now stripped down once again to her natural birthday suit—ran off shrieking for a pest exterminator. As she did so, the quite naked Mrs. Nutbush flapped her limbs and jogged toward the lake looking, thought Mr. Toodles, like a thawed Christmas turkey trying to fly.

The little dachshund turned back and saw that the tiny spotted mutt had run into the hedge with the end of the string, now looped through every item that was formerly on Mrs. Nutbush. The indigo blue and purple head of a much larger pit bull–crayon mix dog emerged from the plants to take the string in its green teeth and pull the tangle of clothes and accessories into the bushes.

Mr. Toodles then watched as a three-legged dachshund and another smaller, curly-haired black mutt approached him through the plants. Sam pointed to the collar and leash around Mr. Toodles's neck. "I'll take that, pal."

Mr. Toodles was too stunned to move.

Sam sighed and nudged Pooft. He spat a flame from his afterburner, charring a tulip six feet behind them.

Mr. Toodles quickly slipped out of the jeweled collar. "Don't kill me," he said, shaking.

Sam and Pooft grabbed the leash in their mouths, turned and ran off down the path along the lake, headed uptown. They were joined by the other depository escapees, Mrs. Nutbush's belongings tumbling behind them on the string like the day's catch of fresh trout.

Then the freshly robbed long-haired little dachshund called out the three most welcome words ever heard during the scrambling raiders' lost, forgotten lives:

"Are you pirates?"

TWENTY-NINE

~ D-DAY ~

Dog Day.

Throngs of people, reporters, TV trucks and police milled about outside of the Madison Square Garden arena, deep in the concrete recesses of Manhattan.

The secretary of the Westminster Kennel Club stood stiffly at the rear entrance, holding a clipboard and staring in horror at a woman in fur walking toward him.

Walking actually isn't a technically accurate term in this case.

Nor *woman*.

If he could have seen below the Peruvian blue vole hat, the leopard fur coat, scarf, glasses, gloves and baby seal boots, he would have seen most of the nervous renegades from the National Last-Ditch Dog Depository clinging to each other like rats on a piece of floating cork.

All were piled atop Fabio, whose spindly legs drove the teetering assembly toward the terrified man.

Bug's face poked up from the fur collar but was largely, gratefully hidden behind the scarf, hat and glasses.

Tied to the woman's empty glove and sleeve was a leash leading down to Sam, trotting nervously in front of her.

But this wasn't the old Sam. Madam had done her makeover magic.

Gone was any evidence of the last three terrible years. The scars and nicks and rips were covered up with the help of bits of fur, glue and the other assorted wonders found in Mrs. Nutbush's makeup kit. Sam's reddish brown coat shone and glistened from the aerosol canola oil found in the trash behind a Waffle House.

And most astounding of all: Sam had four legs again. The steel soup ladle was gone, replaced by a leg made of leather, plastic foam, fur, and the leg bone from a discarded bag of Kentucky Fried Chicken. Sam was again the stunning show dog from his former life.

He had to be. He was the key to getting into this fortress of dog fabulousness.

"I'd wish ya luck, lad . . ." said a familiar Scottish voice. Sam turned to see Peaches in the shadows behind a stall selling Westminster T-shirts. *"I'd wish ya luck if what you*

was doin' was what a dog should be doin'. But it's not. So I won't."

Sam pulled his stumbling "human" toward Peaches.

"I'm setting things right," said Sam.

Peaches sighed. *"Sam the Lion they called ya before. But yer not. Yer a dog. A dog's got twice the heart of a worthless smelly snorin' lion. Yer heart, Sammy. Set that thing right."*

Peaches turned and walked farther into the shadows. Sam was going to call after him, but it was almost noon. Showtime.

Sam held his head high and led the pile of dogs disguised as Mrs. Corinthian Nutbush toward the club secretary at a table covered in white linen, atop which were the badges and numbers that the registered competitors would wear. They stood before the table, the crowd suddenly growing silent around them. Below the coat, the dogs froze, trying not to breathe, burp, whine, itch an ear or break wind.

Which didn't stop Pooft from losing his grip on Ol' Blue's chest and sliding earthward. As the small curly-haired dog tried to regain traction, he slid around toward the rear, giving the full appearance to the observing crowd that below the coat, Mrs. Nutbush's left bosom had gone rogue and begun a migration to better shores.

The club secretary watched this without expression beyond a single perfectly arched eyebrow.

"Madam," he said. "Your bits are restless."

Sam stood up on his rear legs, placed his front paws on the table and offered the Westminster official an ID card, gripped in his teeth. In this case, one from the Vermont Dachshund Club. The man looked at it.

"Mrs. Corinthian Nutbush," he read out loud.

"YES?!" responded another voice from behind the dogs.

Sam, to his horror, turned to see the real Mrs. Nutbush standing several people back in the line. She stomped forward, giving the impression of an irritated refrigerator. "I'M MRS. CORINTHIAN NUTBUSH. WHAT'S THE PROBLEM?"

The real Mrs. Nutbush suddenly recognized her clothes standing next to her. She yelped. "M m my coat! My blue vole hat! These are my clothes! I was robbed yesterday! This thief is an imposter! She's got my boots on backward."

The official turned to the disguised dogs. "I'm terribly sorry to bother you, dear lady . . . but is there any truth to this person's claims?"

Sam froze. The dogs under the clothes began shaking. Sam worried that Pooft would spontaneously erupt with a nervous blast and they would explode like a fireworks display.

"Madam. Are you ill?" the official asked the fake Nutbush. "Can you take your glasses off, please?"

The suspicious man began to reach for the huge sunglasses sitting atop Bug's snout. Behind them, the mutt's huge eyeballs were actually growing even larger and threatened to pop out entirely.

The man glanced down and suddenly froze.

"The Duüglitz tuft!" he whispered. The official reached a shaking hand down and touched the wisp of hair curling up from where Madam had glued it atop Sam's perfect dachshund head.

The official cupped his mouth with a hand and grew pale. He seemed to wilt at the sight of dog greatness, as a church deacon might before the robe of Jesus.

"TH . . . TH-TH-THAT'S MY DUÜGLITZ TUFT!" screamed Mrs. Nutbush.

"Yours?"

"YES!! THAT'S MINE!"

The man sighed with disbelief. "Yes. I'm sure. And so is the Taj Mahal." He snapped his fingers toward some burly men. "Security," he said. The men took Mrs. Nutbush by her arms and began dragging her toward the street. She continued to scream, *"MY DUÜGLITZ!"* even as she was loaded into the back of a police cruiser and driven away for what Sam desperately hoped was the final time. It occurred to Sam that this could only be guaranteed if she were to be shot into space.

"Madam," said the man, turning back to the artificial Mrs. Nutbush and slipping a number 46 around her sleeve, "welcome to the Westminster Dog Show. And may I personally offer you my best wishes for your success."

He bowed.

Fabio—at the bottom of the dog pile and ever the proper one—reflexively did the same.

Bug, atop his shoulders, *did not*.

The hushed crowd watched the northern half of the fake Mrs. Nutbush move in the opposite direction as the southern half as she staggered into the great arena, her various bits again restless and on the move below the leopard coat.

In this fashion did Sam lead his pirate commandos into the greatest dog show on earth in order to destroy it.

Turning back to face the arena hall ahead, Sam immediately smelled Cassius.

THIRTY

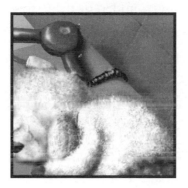

– GO –

Sam hurriedly led the swaying pile of dogs around the arena's perimeter passage to an isolated, latched side exit. Pushing on the door opened it to the alley behind, where the enormous Tusk waited. The huge dog ambled in. Madam jumped on his back.

"There!" Sam pointed to a spiral staircase that disappeared up to the arena's roof far above. "Remember to wait for my signal!"

"Forever, handsome," cooed Madam. Tusk galloped up the stairs toward the roof, Madam hanging on to his back with a cat's nimble balance.

Sam then led his team to the arena's main backstage area. It looked like the pits of the Indianapolis 500, the dozens of racers surrounded by their crews prepping them for the big event. But instead of engines being tuned, it was fur being poofed, nails polished and painted, teeth whitened, noses wiped, eyelashes curled, tails trimmed, breaths sweetened and bottoms perfumed.

The mutts below the fur coat peeked out, eyes wide and disbelieving. They simply had no idea that such creatures existed outside of legend.

"Look," said Ol' Blue, her voice hushed in awe. Never had these unwanted mutts imagined that any dogs could receive so much slavish, smothering, all-consuming devotion from any human being.

This they mistook for love, and it only focused them on the task at hand.

A blast of trumpets startled them. It was the signal for the grand procession of champions. The backstage exploded into a sudden flurry of action, and the dogs and their owners lined up to enter the main arena.

The commandos found a hidden corner behind a support pillar and tumbled forth from the clothing. They moved to a curtain, and each poked out an un-wiped nose to behold the extraordinary sight unfolding inside the cavernous coliseum.

Amidst flashing camera bulbs, men and women led the show dogs in a procession around the arena, circling a central area covered by a vast red carpet. The hundred thousand people in the seats cheered and waved and thundered their approval or disapproval of the canine gladiators strutting before them as they prepared for their battle of beauty. Occasionally, one human would break from the procession and run to the arena's edge and raise his dog above his head before the mob and send them into spasms of hysteria— bewitched as they were by the animal's groomed glory.

On and on the parade of dogs and people went, strutting and prancing and basking in the crowd's passionate roars. Sam scanned the dogs, desperately looking for the huge poodle whose scent even now filled his nostrils, just as its memory filled his thoughts and dreams. He would find Cassius.

And he would kill him.

Or die trying.

The dogs and their owners returned backstage while another blast of trumpets announced the next vital stage in the day's events:

Lunch.

As if called by trainers, the humans streamed out from the backstage area and departed for the miniature sandwich squares at the Grand Breeders Lunch in the terrace, leaving their spoiled champions in their little curtained stalls to do what they did best:

Sleep.

Sam whispered to his commandos: "Get going."

His squad of saboteurs scampered off in all directions and got busy. With paint. Hair gel. Super Glue. Hair dye. Breakfast cereal.

And in Willy and Bug's case, hair clippers.

A fluffy-furred, puffy white prize bichon from Paris snoozed on his grooming table but awoke to a familiar noise. He sleepily looked up to see what he believed to be an enormous hairy potato beetle hanging from the light post above him, with another tiny dog the size of a rodent wrapped in his tongue and dangling just over his body. The rodent dog was holding electric dog clippers and was nearly finished shaving the bichon's body smooth. Except for the buttocks.

The bichon laid his head back down, comforted in the knowledge that he was either dreaming or he was dead and being set upon by demons. Either way, worrying about it was more stress than he was used to and he returned to sleep.

Sam watched with limited interest as his commandos worked . . . for this wasn't why he was really here, of course.

He crept quietly down the aisle of stalls, inspecting the sleeping dogs. Looking. Sniffing.

"Where are you, Cassius, old boy?" whispered Sam, his

heart racing. His nose led him to the final stall, its curtains completely closed, hiding the dog within. He stood poised, unmoving, like a bird dog pointed at its prey.

Suddenly he caught another familiar scent. He knew this one too.

Mrs. Beaglehole.

Sam smelled her dreadful perfume made from the feet of Turkish peahens.

Suddenly the curtains flew open and she appeared, chewing a chicken leg. Sam froze and stared up at her staring down at him only feet away.

The huge woman cocked her head and stopped chewing. *That beautiful dachshund looks familiar.*

They locked eyes. Sam didn't breathe.

"Couldn't be," she said out loud to herself. "You're DEAD!"

She never actually got a chance to say the word *dead,* for when she inhaled her mighty lungs to do so, she sucked the chicken leg into her gaping throat. Grasping at her neck, the choking woman stumbled backward and fell onto the dog bathtub, splintering it into shards of fiberglass while wrenching an ankle made weak from years of supporting more bulk than it was designed for. She belched out a shriek of pain, which shot the chicken leg forth from her mouth like a bazooka, hitting a Persian pekinese in the pooper in the next stall, saving her life but forever traumatizing his.

Sam thought it best to run, which he did, but not before glimpsing the unmistakable puffs of Cassius's white kinky fur as he lay slumbering on a table inside.

Cassius! There! So close . . .

Sam's mind raced . . .

At that same moment, a TV news helicopter circled over the Madison Square Garden arena, reporting on the dog show.

"Lookit that," said the reporter, staring down at the building's roof during a break.

"Lookit what?" said the pilot.

"There's a skinny little mutt on the roof looking through the skylight."

"It's a dog show. He's sneaking a peek." The pilot laughed.

"There's another mutt dragging buckets of dirt from the palm trees up to the water tank and dumping them in."

"Dumping dirt into the water tank?" said the pilot.

"He's making mud," said the reporter. "Wait. Hold it . . ."

He looked again.

"It's a rhinoceros."

THIRTY-ONE

– DANCE –

"Sabotage team, fall back!" whispered Sam, running through the dog stalls moments before the humans returned from lunch. His happy saboteurs poked their heads up from their tasks. The show dogs still napped, professional beauty being exhausting work.

Wee Willy spat out the electric shaver in his mouth. "What's the matter?"

"Get back into the clothes. We're suiting up!"

Bug trotted over to Sam, trying to keep up with him. "We're not finished, Sam."

"Doesn't matter! Change of plans! Let's go!"

"Go and do what?" said Bug, running behind.

Sam and his team disappeared again into the dark corner where they'd left Mrs. Nutbush's things and started piling atop each other below the clothes, putting the poor woman back together once again. Sam slipped the collar over his head, still connected to the leash that was tied to the empty sleeve and glove.

Jeeves pulled himself into the bosom position but stuck a foot into Fabio's ear, making the two-legged mutt jump and sending the lot of them tumbling to the floor in a furred heap.

"C'mon! The others are leaving!" whispered Sam, growing frantic.

"Tell Jeeves my ear is not a footstool," said Fabio. Wee Willy looked out from under the blue vole fur hat as the confused commandos started construction yet again.

"Sam," he said. "What are we doing?"

"Meeting an old friend," said Sam.

Trumpets blew and the lights dimmed in the arena as the crowd roared in anticipation of the final competition . . . and the naming of the grand champion. The judge stood in the center of the red carpet and spoke into the microphone:

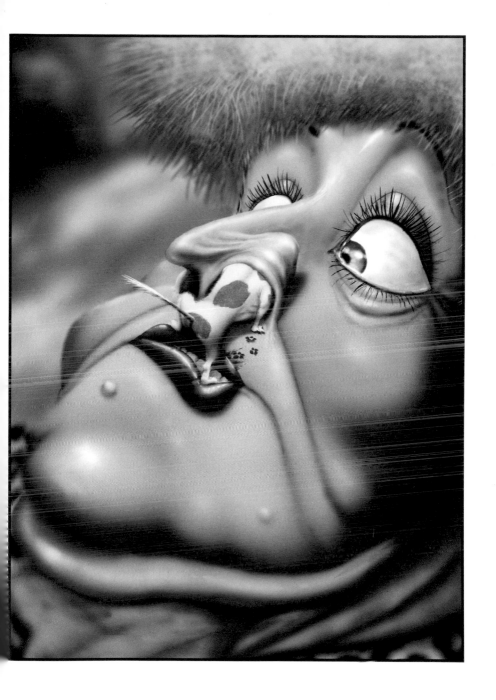

This is when Mrs. Nutbush awoke.

"And now, ladies and gentlemen, the finalists for the Westminster best in show . . . the most beautiful dogs in all the world!"

A roar erupted, shaking the very foundations of the arena. TV cameras swung over to the entrance arch, waiting for the dogs and their owners to emerge.

One by one, the champions trotted out in a processional line with their humans close behind. All shapes, sizes and breeds, they circled the carpet and then took their places surrounding the judge, sitting regally and expectant as the crowd's cheering grew louder.

And then quieter.

And then a complete hush.

Silence.

The crowd had noticed something:

The dogs. Something about them was not quite right *at all.*

The fur of a Bolivian elkhound from France wasn't tan as it should have been. It was lime green. With orange stripes. With little happy faces.

A Spanish shih tzu's lips were dyed hot pink to match his ears, nose and feet.

A Scottish terrier's bottom was striped yellow and black like a bumblebee.

The flowing locks of Britain's favorite sheepdog were strung with beads, plastic army men, and Cheerios.

Those of a collie were worked into rock-hard spikes of

hair gel, pointing in all directions, much like a congealed porcupine.

A miniature poodle's back was shaved smooth of kinky fur. Except for the words I'M WITH THE IDIOT HOLDING THE LEASH.

The dogs—regional national champions all—stared at each other in embarrassed silence.

Someone high in the audience giggled.

Then another. And another.

The laughter then began to build and roll, like a great wave approaching the beach, finally cresting in a thundering crescendo of screaming, howling hoots.

The dogs' owners looked around in horror at the bellowing mob. They'd found their dogs in this condition when they'd returned from lunch. They'd had no time to change anything! Their dogs were a laughingstock.

Except for one.

A lone magnificent poodle.

Cassius.

He sat perfect and unchanged and sublimely gorgeous, watching the others with disgust.

The judge, standing in the middle of the red carpet, recovered from her shock and waved for the crowd to quiet, which they did. Regaining her composure, the judge stiffened, raised her eyebrows and pushed her glasses up her nose. Then she walked to Cassius and waved a single finger to the right. This was the command to begin his judging run, a trot down the short length of carpet and back for a final inspection of form, fur, line and lineage.

Cassius stood and led his human handler down and then back, his head high, his back arched and his tail at exactly a thirty-eight-degree angle.

The crowd hushed.

This was a champion. This was the most beautiful French poodle in the world. As Cassius and his handler returned to his place at the edge of the carpet, the crowd began to applaud.

Cassius beamed. This was going to be his day . . . the place where his whole life had been pointed.

The judge moved toward him. She had only to extend a single index finger over his head and he would be world champion.

High above everything, up on the roof, Madam and Tusk looked down through the skylight . . . waiting for the signal from Sam: the signal for Tusk to ram the south support for the ten-thousand-gallon water tank, causing it to fall forward and land at the edge of the skylight, dumping its now muddy contents through the portal, plummeting down the 150 feet to the red carpet below . . . and onto the heads of the world's most celebrated show dogs sitting on it.

"I can't see Sam!" said Madam, scanning the arena. "Wait. There he is!"

A side curtain at the edge of the show floor parted.

The crowd suddenly went silent again.

The judge, her hand beginning to move toward Cassius, looked up to see a late dachshund competitor moving toward the red carpet, pulling his slower human handler, swaying and stumbling behind him in a leopard skin coat, blue vole hat and baby seal fur boots.

The announcer cleared his throat, his voice booming over the loudspeakers: "Arriving fashionably late is number forty-six, Mrs. Corinthian Nutbush, and her miniature red dachshund, Mr. Toodles."

Sam trotted stiffly in place of Mr. Toodles. But his eyes were locked onto Cassius, who watched him approach with a skeptical, bemused expression. Sam pulled and steered his confused team to the open space next to the huge poodle. He sat down, his eyes never leaving those of Cassius, who stared back, wondering why this dachshund looked vaguely familiar.

He's only feet away, thought Sam, his heart pounding, his mouth dry. He fought to keep his lips from curling upward in rage, revealing his thoughts. *A single leap to the perfectly shaved and perfumed throat. Nobody could stop me.*

Now! he thought. *Your chance is now!*

He glanced upward to Cassius's handler, standing next to the dog he was moments from killing.

It wasn't Mrs. Beaglehole.

In fact, at that moment, Mrs. Beaglehole was sitting with Uncle Hamish in the audience with a heat pack around her ankle and an ice pack around her throat.

Now standing with Cassius was a tall, very nervous-looking young woman with long brown hair pulled back in a neat ponytail and a red bow. She turned and glanced down at Sam.

Sam's blood went cold. He drew a breath and held it, afraid to even release his lungs lest the person in front of him disappear.

This couldn't be real. This he never expected. This he hadn't allowed himself to think about for three years.

Sam scanned the face staring at him and saw that the large brown eyes of a little girl—gleaming with possibility and wonder and wide open to the limitlessness of love—had softened into those of a young woman. These eyes were sadder somehow, thought Sam.

But they were the same.

Heidy.

Heidy.

Sam's head spun. He closed his eyes and then opened them again. It wasn't one of his cruel dreams of a former life he'd tried to forget over the last many years.

No, she was actually there, staring at him, trying like Cassius to make sense of the odd feeling of familiarity they both had about this beautiful dachshund.

From below the leopard coat, Ol' Blue whispered to Fabio underneath his fanny: "What's wrong with Sam?"

Fabio shrugged, which nearly toppled the lot of them.

"Number forty-six, Mr. Toodles, and his owner, Mrs. Corinthian Nutbush, please make your judging run," said the judge, suddenly clearing Sam's swimming head. Sam looked around. Everyone was watching him, waiting, hushed.

For Sam, suddenly the thought of killing Cassius—the thought that had dominated all others for a week—was replaced by another:

Heidy. Once lost . . . *she might be his again.*

She stared down at him. *What was she waiting for?*

Suddenly he knew.

She was waiting to see the old Sam the Lion.

He stepped onto the red carpet, pulling his "Mrs. Nutbush," causing them to stumble and sway.

"Sam! What're we doing?" whispered Bug from below the fur hat.

But Sam was too lost in the memories from a previous time to answer. He pulled his team to the center of the carpet as the judge and Heidy and Cassius and a hundred thousand people in the arena and millions around the world watched.

Then he stopped. He looked back at Heidy, still staring with a quizzical expression . . .

And then he danced. Just as he and a little girl had done in the Vermont backyard of McCloud Acres a lifetime ago. He leapt and twirled and bounced, his mind suddenly awash in a feeling approaching happiness . . . one that he hadn't dared allow for a very long time.

Cassius stared . . . awash in his own memories: *I've seen this before.*

Heidy was thinking the same thing . . . but her mind couldn't make sense of it. Sam was gone. Destroyed years ago when she was a little girl. *Dogs don't return from the dead.*

In the audience, Uncle Hamish stood, staring, disbelieving.

The crowd began laughing again at the dancing, spinning dachshund. They hadn't seen such a performance at a dog show before . . . but the dachshund was quite beautiful.

But then suddenly a hush fell upon the arena.

"The . . . The Duüglitz Tuft!" someone cried out in the audience.

More people pointed and shouted: "The Duüglitz!"

Outstretched fingers shot toward the top of Sam's skull, pointing at the tiny curled wisp of hair that Sam had instructed Madam to glue atop his head.

"The Duüglitz Tuft . . ." the judge said in a whispered awe, her eyes brimming with tears. She picked up the huge silver best in show chalice and blue championship ribbon and began to move toward the heartbreakingly flawless dachshund.

A thunderous cheer then arose from the now standing, fist-pumping, astonished crowd. *The DUÜGLITZ!!*

Sam the Lion was cookin'! He was on fire! The roars and cheers drove his spinning and bouncing to a frenzied pace and he twirled and danced and flipped and . . .

And then it was suddenly quiet again.

Sam stopped. The crowd was standing, staring, mute. He looked over at Heidy, who stared but held a hand to her open mouth.

He looked around on the red carpet. Pieces of fur and leather and tape and glue lay scattered. His artificial leg lay several feet away from him.

Sam stood, leaning slightly on his three feet, ragged and shorn of his deceit. He blinked . . . as if waking from a rapturous daydream.

But it was not a dream.

High atop the roof, Tusk and Madam stared down through the open skylight at the events unfolding below. "Oh, dear," said Madam very simply.

Watching from the edge of the red carpet, suddenly Cassius knew. He suddenly saw everything clearly. The big poodle leapt forward, snapping the leash held by Heidy. He reached the backside of the fake Mrs. Nutbush, still teetering close to Sam . . .

. . . and he sunk his teeth into her bottom.

Which was actually Ol' Blue's. Which started a predictable chain reaction of dogs tumbling hard down onto the red carpet into a tangled heap of squirming mutt bodies, coats, hats, legs, boots and tails.

Heidy walked toward the tangle of ridiculous dogs and the one battered, very flawed but familiar dachshund at the center. She picked up the fake leg . . . and felt the pieces of fur that had been pasted over his scars. Her head spun.

"No . . ." she said and backed away, confused, trying to make sense of the unbelievable.

Sam watched her move backward. *"What's wrong? Heidy, it's me. It's Sam. I'm here! It's ME!"*

"But it's not you," said Cassius, again approaching his old enemy. *"Look at yourself. You're not the dog she loved before. You're broken. You're ugly. I told you before and it's still true: she doesn't want you now."*

Sam looked at Heidy and saw the confusion in her face.

Sam suddenly believed Cassius's lie.

"Run, stray, run," said the big poodle.

Sam did. He dashed for the exit at the far end of the arena.

"Sam!" cried Heidy, but he didn't hear her.

But Cassius did. And in her voice, the one he'd learned to know and love more than any during the last many years, the poodle heard what he dreaded: she still loved the dachshund.

Far more than she'd ever love him.

Cassius dashed after the running Sam. He knew he had to do what he should have done years before to keep Heidy in his life.

He had to kill him.

The vast crowd of onlookers was blocking the exits, and Sam turned around to see Cassius almost on him, a look of fury in his eyes. Sam's will for vengeance was broken, his spirit collapsed, and he only wanted out, out, *out*.

Cassius was on him and they both fell against a tangle of folding chairs, sending the crowd screaming. Sam pulled out from the jaws of the big poodle and his old survival instincts took over:

Head for higher ground. Go *up*.

A steep set of circular steps pointed toward the steel rafters of the ceiling . . . and the giant boxes that hung from them, the ones used as scoreboards during sporting events. Sam shot up the stairs, the lack of a fourth leg slowing him only slightly. Cassius followed, only seconds behind Sam, his teeth bared in furious hatred.

"Sam! Sam the Lion!" screamed Heidy, who reached the stairs just as both dogs ascended above her. She followed them up before the show officials could stop her.

Close behind her, the entire commando squad from the National Last-Ditch Dog Depository scrambled to catch up.

They had no idea why. But they were a team, and it seemed right to follow Sam, if not totally sensible. They stumbled and scrambled up the stairs, snapping at the hands of officials trying to stop them.

As the stunned crowd craned their necks and the TV cameras pointed up at the remarkable events occurring high above the red carpet, only one thing remained clear for them and the millions of people watching around the world:

This was the best Westminster ever.

THIRTY-TWO

- NOW -

Sam reached the top of the stairs, the arena ceiling blocking further ascent. Cassius was nearly there himself. Sam looked around for escape. A single narrow steel catwalk stretched the length of the ceiling, reaching the huge, angled score boxes hanging from the center of the roof, just below the skylight. Sam dashed across. Cassius reached the girders himself and followed.

Heidy was close behind. She looked down to the distant floor and all the people staring up like ants and she had to fight off dizziness. She sucked in a deep breath and started moving across the spidery walkway toward Sam and Cassius.

Sam reached the score boxes and leapt to the top of the first one of the four, each pointed slightly downward toward the seats in different directions. He lost his footing and nearly slid off, his rear foot at the edge.

The red carpet was directly below, almost two hundred feet.

Cassius landed several yards in front of him, facing him straight on. His voice was calm. Cold. Cruel. And familiar. *"It's time, dear, departed Sam. Three years later . . . and you're in the same place, aren't you, old boy? Another broken, lost, unwanted stray. Just take a single step backward and make things simple. It's so easy. You did it before."*

Cassius was right, thought Sam. There was nothing left. No reason to keep going, really. No purpose remaining. There was that word for a dog again. Purpose.

Do I have one left now? Sam thought.

He looked down to the floor far below. Stepping off would be easy.

"Cassius," said a voice behind them. They both turned to see Heidy on the box with them, crouched on her hands and knees. Cassius's heart sank as he saw the look on her face. A look of coldness and contempt. "Cassius . . . it was always you, wasn't it? You took the baby. You turned us against Sam. It was you."

Suddenly, the great beautiful show dog knew that his life could never be the same now that Heidi knew. She would hate him. Fear him. Resent him. And finally, he would become that which no dog can ever really endure:

Unwanted.

And in that same instant, Cassius's heart took the full impact and it did what all dog hearts can do, whether bright or dark, warm or cold, pure or foul:

It broke.

Cassius turned toward Heidy, his lips curled into a new and different rage. His wrath was now upon *her.* He lowered his perfectly groomed head and moved toward the young woman. Fear swept Heidy's face and she crawled backward . . . but had nowhere to go.

Cassius bent his long legs low, ready to spring toward Heidy with muscles taut. He opened his jaws.

But Sam leapt first.

With a guttural scream, the small dachshund was suddenly upon him from behind, wrapping his long jaws tightly around the perfectly shaved neck while he wrapped his front legs around the poodle's frizzy chest. They fell on their side, teeth flashing and jaws snapping, their legs and feet kicking the air and each other in a blurred frenzy of violent movement.

Far below, the crowd screamed, too stunned to move.

The announcer on the loudspeakers urged calm until order could be returned.

Order was not close to returning.

The flailing dogs caused Heidy to move backward and slip off the large score box, falling six feet to a smaller box hanging below, holding the clock. Her feet then lost their purchase on the smooth surface and she slid off this, catching herself to keep from falling to her death by a weak grasp on the single brace of aluminum with a single hand.

In the roaring audience Hamish stared up in horror at his niece. Mrs. Beaglehole sat next to him, mouth agape, words stuck in her bovine throat like a chicken leg.

Sam's commando squad of mutts watched the fighting dogs and the now-dangling Heidy from the catwalk fifty feet away at the edge of the arena ceiling. Ol' Blue saw a large coil of thin rope, used to pull up crates of replacement bulbs for the scoreboard. He picked it up in his teeth and dropped half of it to the floor far below. Several men ran to it and grasped it, since that's what humans seem to do when faced with a dangling rope.

Ol' Blue faced Pooft. "How's the digestion today, top gun?" Blue asked. Pooft looked down at the floor hundreds of feet below and then back at the blue dog.

"Troublesome," he said. This was good news.

Blue turned to Jeeves. "Good day to fly, pal."

"Why not?" said the hound.

She turned to the six-ounce Willy. "Willy, secure the goods."

"Right," said the tiny terrier.

With that, Pooft hopped onto Jeeves's back and lay down, much as a jet engine might sit atop a Cessna. Willy took the rope end in his mouth and did what a pair of hands might have: zip around the two dogs, building a hasty but effective harness that strapped them tightly together. Ol' Blue pointed the two of them at Heidy, still dangling and close to losing her grip. Bug and Fabio steadied the catwalk and made sure the rope was clear.

"Ignition," said Blue.

The explosive blast suddenly hushed the crowd below. High above their heads, they watched two inelegant mutts rocket off the end of the catwalk on a small but explosive burst of flaming gas from poorly digested kibble. Maintaining altitude with the help of wing-like jowls, they sailed just over the head of the young woman hanging from the clock box and then plunged earthward, their momentum and fuel exhausted.

They dropped only a few feet since the rope grew taut across the clock box framework and was held firm by the men far below. The dogs dangled, as a very heavy kite might from a very high tree.

As targeted, the rope lay within inches of Heidy's free hand. She grasped the line and held on, her feet wrapping around the rope.

Slowly, the men on the ground fed out their end of the rope and lowered the entire group to the red carpet two hundred feet below.

Heidy pushed away from Uncle Hamish, who'd rushed to help her. She looked back up at the dogs still fighting to the death above their heads.

"SAM! SAM!" she yelled, but the crowd was too loud for her voice to carry.

High overhead, caught in Cassius's death grip, Sam's strength was giving out. Blood streamed from tooth punctures, and his flesh was ripped across his back from manicured nails. Cassius held a fold of his neck in his teeth, slowly suffocating the small dog. Sam—on his back—pushed against the big poodle with paws too short. He had only enough breath to croak out a final question in a whispered rasp.

"Someday   somewhere . . . you're going to kill her too, aren't you?"

"Yes," said Cassius, whispering through the teeth clenched on Sam's neck. "If she won't love me."

"She won't," said Sam.

Sam moved his eyes up past the reddening face of Cassius and saw Tusk and Madam staring down in horror at him through the roof skylight.

"Now!" called out Sam, despite the jaws that pulled his neck.

Madam stared down. She thought she'd heard him say the word, but couldn't believe it. It would kill them.

"Now," said Sam again, mustering up the last shreds of his strength. "NOW!"

On the roof, Madam turned to her huge partner and yelled, "Now, Tusk! Do it now!"

Tusk turned and leapt. His full weight hit the fourth leg

of the water tank support, buckling it. The tank groaned as the other steel legs bent and broke and finally gave way to gravity. As Tusk and Madam dove to safety, the round tank landed flat on its side, bursting its roof with a cannon shot explosion, releasing its ten thousand gallons of pudding-like mud onto the skylight. The glass shattered and the liquid burst through like a brown waterfall, hitting the top of the score boxes just below it. Cassius never knew what it was that slammed into them, carrying both dogs over the edge and falling, tumbling, spinning to the never-to-be-clean-again red carpet two hundred feet below.

THIRTY-THREE

– RISEN –

Women screamed and men yelled as the tens of thousands of spectators erupted in panic and rushed to the exits. The gooey cascade of mud raining down from the heavens had stopped, but many guessed that other biblical plagues might follow and it'd be smart to leave before the locusts came.

Dozens of the world's most beautiful dogs shook off

the bulk of the mud that coated their bodies and staggered away from the arena center in a sort of muddled daze.

All but two.

Two figures lay prone and unmoving at the center of the vast mud-covered floor as people and dogs swirled in chaos about the edge.

Heidy, coated in the brown ooze herself, slowly walked past the unmoving form of Cassius and approached the small dachshund lying next to him. She dropped to her knees next to Sam and gently picked him up with both hands. Sam's head hung to the side. She cradled the limp dog and looked down at the brown eyes she had thought she'd never see again and her shoulders slumped with a sadness beyond simple grief. A sadness made even more hollow by regret. Regret that she hadn't believed in him when he'd needed it most, years ago. Regret that she would now never have the chance to tell him how sorry she was for this. Regret for the seasons unspooled, the birthdays celebrated, the happy, small moments of a life passed unshared by the dog that just gave her his.

She wept, but made no sound.

And then neither she nor anyone else in that frantic arena noticed that time seemed to have come to a stop. The lights dimmed, and a darkness dropped over everything. The walls, the sounds and the people faded into the background, as if suddenly out of focus. A blue light, shimmering down, like moonbeams underwater, fell on Heidy—

quiet and unmoving, her head bowed—Sam still held tight in her arms.

A figure walked in slowly from the surrounding darkness and sat next to them and looked at Sam with a slight smile. If Sam could have seen, he would have recognized the preposterous terrier–hyena–dust mop mix.

Peaches.

"Poor Sammy. You've had a rough go of it, lad."

Peaches looked up into Heidy's mud-splattered face, still bowed.

"Aye, she's a good one, she is. Worth fighting for. Or dying for, eh, Sam?"

The little dog studied Sam's face, his eyes closed, his great heart stilled.

"You lost it for a bit. The thing that we're here for. But in the end you found it again, didn't ya, lad? A shame to waste such a fine thing, it is."

He paused.

"Sure enough, Sam. Your last day will come. . . ."

Peaches turned, stretched his lumpy frame and yawned. The most unexpected of angels turned and walked away toward the darkness outside the blue light and said without looking back:

". . . but it's not this one, laddie."

Sam opened his eyes.

He saw only a blurry image just beyond his long nose. As his head cleared, he saw that the fuzzy shape was the face of a young woman, smeared with dirt and tears, her eyes closed. An old instinct returned without him thinking about it, as instincts do . . . and he licked just below her nose.

Heidy opened her eyes, startled, and looked down at her dog. She blinked. Sam did the same. She pulled Sam up and tucked his muddy snout tight into her neck as she so often had in the past. She waited for the warmth of his breath and it came and she knew that it wasn't a dream. She closed her eyes again and whispered into his torn ear:

"Sam. You've come home."

Sam's dog commandos sat several feet away and looked at each other with something like astonishment. Then they watched the young woman stand up, still holding Sam, and move toward an exit. Uncle Hamish slipped next to her, leaving Mrs. Beaglehole staring and stunned, still seated in the VIP section, where she may still be today.

The crowd of pushing, shoving people suddenly calmed. They moved apart, making a clear path for the young woman and the three-legged dachshund. Before entering the bright light of the afternoon sun, Heidy turned and looked back into the arena. She looked at Sam's commandos, sitting in the mud watching her along with everyone else. She held out an open hand toward them.

"Aren't you coming?" she said.

And then before the thousands of hushed people in the audience and the millions of stunned viewers watching across the world on TV . . . the flawed and muddied depositees of the National Last-Ditch Dog Depository followed Heidy and Sam and quietly filed out of the Westminster Dog Show, noses held high, backs straight, mud glistening.

Wee Willy, sitting on Tusk's butt with tiny tail waving, turned to look at the passing crowd.

"Drink up, me hearties, yo ho!" he said.

THIRTY-FOUR

- LION -

Vermont.

Ol' Blue led the flawed dogs as they discovered what a field of autumn dandelions will do when a pack of mutts tear into it. Streaking across the hills, they and another fifty barking beasts also discovered that while catching dandelion wisps in dramatic balletic leaps could be fun, digesting them was not. Pooft discovered this earlier and the Piddleton fire department had to retrieve him from the singed upper branches of the valley's tallest maple tree.

As the dogs ran ahead, Uncle Hamish lay on his back sunning himself in a small wagon, his head on Violett's lap. Bruno, now four, sat in front, holding the reins. Tusk—the only one of the original flawed commandos still un-adopted—wore a harness and pulled the lot of them up the hill after the other dogs, his momentum maintained by a giggling Bruno chucking stale baguettes out in front of the happy, huge beast.

Coming in last was Heidy, strolling in the tall grass while Sam stretched atop her head and chewed a dandelion stalk. At the crest of the hill, they could see down to the manor house and kennels, newly renamed the McCloud Heavenly Acres Shelter for Peopleless Dogs.

Heidy and Sam watched several cars pull up, the first of the day. Kids tumbled out and pointed toward the mutts making their way down the hill toward them. Tusk stopped and sat down shyly before a very small, very skinny ten-year-old boy, who stared up at him, arms stiff at his sides.

"There are," said the boy matter-of-factly, "some kids at my bus stop that grab the Ho Hos from my lunch sack every day."

Tusk looked at the boy's father standing behind him, who shrugged.

"Not anymore," said Tusk.

The boy turned and sat down between the dog's huge

legs and lay back into the furry chest, his head fitting neatly below the long chin. He looked up at his dad with a grin. "This one."

Sam watched his commandos meet their human visitors—just as varied and imperfect and splendidly flawed as the dogs were—and he knew that here, love would have a better chance to find its way, as it usually does with dogs.

Sam noticed something else. A pickup truck had stopped and a young man had gotten out. The truck was new . . . and the nice clothes were not familiar . . . but the man was.

Sam dropped to Heidy's shoulders, then to the ground. He loped down the hill on his three legs until he got close enough to the visitor to know that the man's hands were probably a bit less rough now. He approached, and the man knelt down low to do what Sam had never allowed him to do before: gently stroke the top of his head.

"So, little buddy. It's Sam the Lion now, is it?" the man said.

"*Always was,*" said Sam, and he closed his eyes.

"Aye, she's a good one, she is, Sam.
Worth fighting for. Worth dying for."